ON THE HARD DODGE

It was crazy, Jackson thought. Why hadn't they let him reach the canyon, ride right into their ambush? He looked back toward the canyon and understood. A slender column of smoke rose from the canyon—its meaning as crisp as semaphore. It told the possemen below that he was here.

These were disciplined men following strict orders. They were not to take him. He was being hunted as a trophy animal is hunted, with an entourage of scouts and beaters to maneuver the prey into the sights of the privileged hunter who would make the kill. Jackson laughed softly.

"Can't plan much ahead now," he told the buckskin. "We've got to get out of this valley. Do the best you can for me, old soldier."

07-09

CATCH PARTY
WILLIAM O. TURNER

ZEBRA BOOKS
KENSINGTON PUBLISHING CORP.

ZEBRA BOOKS

are published by

Kensington Publishing Corp.
475 Park Avenue South
New York, NY 10016

First printing: April, 1988

Printed in the United States of America

PROLOGUE

The real estate man sits on the steps of the lonely little ranchhouse, studying a plan of the new subdivision. He rolls it up and gets to his feet as the slick-sculptured, late model Mercedes glides to a stop. He bustles forward to greet the man and the leggy girl in jeans.

The man is white haired and into his late fifties. The girl is in her early teens, his granddaughter. The man looks at the house appreciatively. When he last saw it, it was rickety and neglected. Now it has been mended and painted a soft red with white trim. It looks old but tidy and solid.

It's in a place where it won't interfere with the installation of water and sewer lines, the real estate man says, and the company will use it as an on-site sales office. When the lots are all sold, well, they'll probably doze it down then. The plan calls for a little landscaped triangle here. Shrubbery, a rock garden, a tasteful redwood sign with the name of the new community on it. Windsong Acres. How about that? This is a class operation right down to the smallest detail.

The small pigskin steamer trunk that the electricians found under the rafters has been brought down to the porch. It has been wiped off and is in good condition. Undoubtedly a valuable antique, the real estate man says. Surprising, what you can get for old stuff like that. But this is clearly something of sentimental value. High Plains Developments is pleased to turn it over to the family as a courtesy. Of course, he says, he is curious to know what's inside. If there are old abstracts, surveys, or anything like that, the legal department would be pleased to see them. He was tempted to force the lock, he admits, but it would be a shame to damage a fine old piece like that.

The girl is on her knees. She has found a six-inch scrap of stout copper wire and she inserts it into the lock.

"There's a locksmith in town," the real estate man says, "at the hardware store."

"She has a talent for things like this," the man says. "A natural born snoop."

"This sucker should be easy," the girl says. She inserts the wire into a crack in the porch floor in order to bend the tip. Then she lays it over the porch rail and bends it in the middle to give her a grip and leverage. Returning to the lock, she points to faded letters on the round top of the trunk, initials. "He was your grandfather?"

"Yes," the man says. "Your great-great."

"You remember him?"

"Barely. He died—it must have been in the late twenties. I would have been six or seven."

"A locksmith will have the proper tools," the real estate man says. "He'll know exactly how to—"

6

"What was he like?" the girl says.

The man is squinting, peering into memory. "I remember sitting on his lap once, and he smelled good. Tobacco and something else. Witch hazel, I think. I don't remember much else except that he was always writing. He was always sitting off to himself and scribbling in one of those old five-cent composition books."

"Bingo!" the girl says.

"I'll be darned," the real estate man says.

They raise the lid gently, the man catching it and holding it upright so it won't strain the hinges. The staleness, faintly tinged with camphor, is overpowering, the casually encapsulated atmosphere of another world.

The girl lifts out clothing and shakes it out. An old black suitcoat gone greenish. A blue Civil War tunic with sergeant's chevrons. The man identifies a strangely shaped wooden device as a bootjack. A cigar box contains collar buttons, cuff links, a cigar clip, a buttonhook, a razor, a sheriff's badge. A heavy oilskin bundle turns out to hold a Colt revolver—a real treasure, the real estate man says. Under all the other stuff, covering the entire bottom of the small trunk, there is a six-inch layer of composition books. . . .

I

The Journal of Patrick H. Briley, Sheriff of Hooper County, Montana.

Hooper City, Hooper County, Mont., Sunday, June 9, 1901, 12:15 A.M.

S. Swanson, night clerk at Primrose Hotel, was pistol-whipped and is in doctor's office in a coma, maybe dying. H. Yates, a one-armed horse trader, was robbed and thrown from second story of said hotel, Room 29, which didn't do him any good either. He is ambulatory and refuses medical attention except for whiskey. He states the following facts and allegations, near as I can piece it together:

He arrived here three days ago with a small string of horses, mostly cobs, and a French-Canadian wrangler. His camp is just south of town, and he has been engaged in commerce and barter there, although he spends nights at the hotel. My office has received a few complaints of misrepresentation, et cetera, from the public but no more than usual in horse-trading situations.

Yates spent evenings playing stud poker at the Happy Pilgrim, a saloon. Due to his presence and that of another stranger, known as Jackson, the game tonight got heavy. There were several pots of several hundred dollars each. I was personally present and saw the last hand played. (I was not a player.)

Yates was dealer. As was his custom, he passed the cards to another player to be shuffled. Then he dealt one-handed. Jackson, who had been losing, bet big and Yates raised. The other players dropped out early. Jackson and Yates kept raising each other on every card, and there must have been close to $1000 in that pot. Yates won with a king full.

Jackson, who had a ten full, accused Yates of cheating. He couldn't back up the accusation in any way, but he wanted me to arrest Yates anyhow. How could I charge a one-armed man with cardsharping?

Yates left the saloon. Jackson had a drink at the bar and also left. According to Yates, Jackson then busted into his hotel room. He coldcocked the clerk, who tried to interfere, took Yates's money at gunpoint, and expelled him through the window, which was in a closed position. Damage estimated at $1 for a new pane plus 50¢ labor.

Yates states that he was robbed of $3,410.00 in greenbacks and $80.00 in gold, this being not only his gambling money but also the capital of his horse-trading business and his life savings.

He is now at the Happy Pilgrim and is somewhat overwrought from the effects of his loss, a possible concussion, and from whiskey. He has posted a signed notice pledging a 20% reward for the return of his money. This figures out to be $698.00.

Due to his generous offer and to the fact that the onset occurred on a Saturday night with spring roundup just over and the saloons full, the public is in a state of excitement. A sizable pursuit party has assembled. It is now at the Pilgrim, discussing tactics and trying to figure out in which direction Jackson took flight.

This town is only a few miles south of the county line and the Pioneer Fathers made a damnfool mistake when they laid out the boundaries. Anybody who is in trouble here can get into Bannock County and out of my jurisdiction in less than an hour. In my opinion, that is what Jackson has done, but in its present state of excitement the public won't listen to me. I have dispatched a deputy to notify Sheriff Hornbill at Sperrysville of the situation, there being no direct telephone line. You can get a connection by way of Idaho Falls, Butte, and Helena, but it takes three hours, you can't hear clear, and Hornbill is deaf anyway.

The pursuit party consists of an estimated 25 souls, an estimated 90% of which are drunk. There is no way I can discourage pursuit, not with that kind of reward posted, even though it won't amount to much if divided by 25. Best I can do is deputize the whole kettle and boiling, ride along, and try to keep the citizens from shooting up the first lone rider they come across.

Sperrysville, Bannock County. Same day. 4:45 A.M.
After some circumbendulating, looking for Jackson's trail by lantern, I persuaded the party that he likely as not went straight up the stage road to this town, which it turned out he did. Meanwhile the

party lost several souls on the trail due to digestive upsets, mental confusion, et cetera. One, who was seeing luminescent leprechauns and was firing at them, I disarmed. Sent him back to Hooper in company of the town barber, who had sobered up and was tired of the whole ranikiboo.

Jackson arrived here well ahead of my messenger, it seems. He traded his horse at the livery, along with $20 boot money, for a big blue roan and continued on his way, apparently in a northerly direction.

When my deputy arrived with news of a fugitive on the loose, he foolishly mentioned the reward. Sheriff Hornbill, an excitable man, couldn't wait to announce this to the public before the last saloons closed. Word spread fast and Sperrysville is undergoing the same confusion we had at Hooper, with Hornbill right in the middle of it. When we got here, he was forming up a party with the idea of riding south, by what reasoning I don't know. It wasn't until I arrived that the liveryman woke up and told us that a man answering Jackson's description had been here and was pointed on up the road on a fresh horse.

The country north of here is grass and sage with the St. Terry River slipping along the east edge of it. Up to there it is fairly flat, but just beyond the river the War Bonnets rise up sudden. They are a narrow range of big buttes tangled up with some ragged foothills with narrow canyons and large rocky valleys cutting into them. If Jackson swings east and gets into them, this is likely to be a long, hard manhunt. With this in mind, I got a restaurant proprietor out of bed, name of Sun Lee, a Celestial, and persuaded him to cook ham and eggs for some of

11

my party. However, many continued to paint their tonsils along with the local citizenry.

The men I deputized have volunteered for Hornbill's party and have got swore in all over again. There has been a delay occasioned by somebody throwing a bottle in the air and firing at it, killing Hornbill's horse, but the combined parties are now mounting up. Hornbill has made no request for my presence, but I will ride along to keep the lid on the best I can.

The clamjamphrie now consists of an estimated 45 souls. I estimate that 30% of the horses and 40% of the men will exflunctify within 15 miles.

II

Dressed for church in a pale serge skirt and jacket, tiny straw hat pinned to graying hair, Mrs. Snyder was feeding her chickens. The posse had encircled the ranch buildings and it exploded into the yard in an eruption of dust and white leghorns. Too terrified even to scream, Mrs. Snyder gaped as men leaped from saddles and, weapons in hand, swept into the barn, the bunkhouse, and the house.

They prodded the three ranch hands from the bunkhouse, one of them in longjohns. Her husband came around a corner of the house, his hands raised. He was followed by a tall, loose-coupled man who waved a huge revolver.

"Found this one in the privy!" the man yelled. "He fit the description, Sheriff?"

A small, glary-eyed man on a paint horse swung toward the pair, and Mrs. Snyder recognized Sheriff Hornbill. Another mounted man rode over, too, a big, gray-haired, square-built man. After a hard look at him, she decided he was Sheriff Briley of Hooper County.

"That's Andy Snyder you got there," Briley said.

13

"Hell yes, you tarnal idiot!" Hornbill yelled. He was deaf, Mrs. Snyder remembered, deaf and excitable, and he always yelled. "He's the owner of this ranch and a law-abiding citizen! Good morning, Andy."

The man behind Snyder lowered the revolver. Mrs. Snyder rushed over to stand beside her husband.

"My apologies, folks!" Hornbill yelled. "The boys is a little honed up. We're on the track of a desper-ay-do. He could have concealed himself hereabouts, so we got to search!"

Realizing he was no longer held at gunpoint, Mr. Snyder lowered his hands, buttoned his fly, and recovered his self-confidence. He turned on the man who had captured him.

"There must be something in the Constitution of the United States of America that protects a citizen's right to use his privy of a Sunday morning without being rousted out by some clown who has drunk too much of the red disturbance. What's your name?"

"Schrockenmeyer." The man holstered the huge revolver, looking as if he expected Snyder to shake hands.

"Your full name! I want to know who to sue."

"You can't do it!" Hornbill yelled. "This here is a posse comitatus and—"

"A what?" Snyder demanded.

"A catch party," Sheriff Briley put in.

"There was a crime committed in Briley's county!" Hornbill yelled. "The desper-ay-do took flight into this here county, where he has been criss-crossing every which way over the back country. So what we have here is a two-county posse comitatus, citizens

14

obliged to cooperate, and I will brook no talk of anybody whatsoever suing anybody else whatsoever!"

Snyder was a churchgoing man who tried to avoid profanity, but his words rang out loud and clear. "Jesus Christ and J. Pierpont Morgan! To think I voted for you!"

The thought of losing a vote brought a change in Hornbill's attitude. He aimed his glare at Briley. "Sheriff, I'd appreciate it if you'd keep a rein on your Hooper County yahoos!"

"If you wasn't so excitable," Briley said, "you'd recognize this particular yahoo as a member of the Bannock County branch of the Schrockenmeyer family. Maybe you just lost *two* votes."

A rider raced up and pulled to a skidding stop in a blast of dust. He yelled to Hornbill that it looked like they'd picked up the fugitive's trail. "He's headed east, pointed for the river! Looks like he's changed horses again."

Mrs. Snyder took her husband by the arm and led him to the porch steps. There were two wicker chairs on the porch, occupied now by an exhausted posseman and a white leghorn. Mrs. Snyder stopped suddenly on the top step.

"Great day, Andy! Laura Jean!"

"Great day!" Snyder echoed, clapping a hand to his cheek. He turned to call to Hornbill.

"Laura Jean left here just before daybreak, headed east! She's all alone. On her way to Langtown."

Hornbill swung his mount closer to the porch. He cupped a hand to his ear.

"Who?"

"The Dundee girl. She's been living with us since

her mother died. She just graduated from high school and she's got herself a job up there."

"Up where?"

"Langtown!" Snyder yelled impatiently. "She's on a pinto mare. She—"

"That's an eighty mile ride!" Hornbill yelled.

"She plans to take the night at my brother's place near Table City."

"She on the stage road?"

"She's shortcutting. Headed east."

The sheriff nodded curtly and reined away.

"She's dressed in pants!" Mrs. Snyder yelled after him, not at all sure that he heard. "Don't mistake her for the desper-ay-do!"

"That's not likely," Snyder said. "She's also wearing a sunbonnet."

"This passel of lunatics might not notice," Mrs. Snyder said.

They watched the party mount in a confusion of whirling horses and stream out of the yard, its wake a boiling plume. Wagging his head sadly, Snyder turned to go into the house. His wife caught his arm and pointed to one of their ranch hands, who was approaching the house in a straddle-legged run.

"Old Red ain't in the pasture, Mr. Snyder! Looks like somebody borried him."

Snyder took a deep breath, closing his eyes, smothering cusswords.

"Whoever took him left their own horse behind," the man added.

"That horn-voiced little stub-runt of a sheriff is responsible for the doings of his possemen! I'll make him pay through the nose. There must be something

16

in the Constitution of the United States—"

Afraid that her husband was going to swear again, Mrs. Snyder cut him off. "Maybe a posse comitatus has the right to requisition livestock," she said. "But the sheriff is supposed to give you a receipt or something. They didn't even have the courtesy to tell us about it. Great day, Andy! What if . . . ?"

"What if what?"

"What if it wasn't a posseman who took Red?"

"Great day!"

"It ain't a bad horse that was left behind," the ranch hand said. "Big blue roan. Only thing wrong with him, he's got a loose shoe."

III

It was what Laura Jean Dundee thought of as a blue-eyed morning. The sun had inched over the War Bonnet peaks, splashing them with gold where they were still veined with snow. There was the smell of sage in the air and the challenge of distance to cover, and the feel of a new beginning. Later it would be hot, but now there was a soft breeze with a tingle in it that made her horse want to canter and Laura Jean went to whistle. She trilled out "Listen to the Mockingbird" for a while and then switched to "Camptown Races" with variations.

She was riding a pinto mare named Flag that belonged to her older brother, Timbo. He had left it with her last week when he came down from Langtown to try for a loan from the Sperrysville bank and to attend her graduation exercises. She was wearing high-button shoes, overalls, a man's shirt with a yellow silk scarf wrapped around her neck over the collar band, and a sunbonnet. Her saddle was a decrepit old McClellan Timbo had provided.

Mr. and Mrs. Snyder, the dears, had been appalled to learn that she meant to undertake a two-day journey alone and, of all things, *astride* a horse. To call it undecorous, they insisted, was putting it mildly. They had gone on and on about it, citing such undecorous female astride riders as Cattle Kate, Belle Starr, Calamity Jane, and some hussies they themselves had seen in Pawnee Bill's Wild West Show when they were back east in Chicago six years ago. The last had worn split riding skirts, which struck Laura Jean as a good idea but which the Snyders considered even more scandalous than pants. *Provocative* was the word they used.

She had finally challenged them to give her one *specific* reason, aside from sheer prudishness, why a female shouldn't sit a horse the way a male does. She knew there was a rather devastating answer to that but she also knew that the Snyders, bless their Presbyterian hearts, were incapable of that kind of specificity. The tactic embarrassed them almost to the point of speechlessness. While they didn't entirely drop their protest, their hearts were no longer in it, and here she was.

"We shall be judged undecorous by all whom we encounter," she told the mare. "But we don't really have much choice. I had to sell my sidesaddle to help pay for Mother's funeral. Besides, I am saving six dollars and fifty cents stage fare, you are a very good horse, and I am enjoying the trip, even though I'm going to be sore as Job's pet boil by nightfall. Anyhow, we don't give two bangs on a tin pan how people judge us, do we?"

A meadowlark sounded off and she whistled back at him and then took off on "Buffalo Gal." The horse enjoyed her whistling. She knew that without

19

knowing how she knew it, and she reflected on the strange rapport between horse and rider that is especially acute when they are alone in open country. It was almost telepathic, she concluded.

A few minutes later it was the horse that alerted her to the rider behind them. Aware that the animal sensed something that she did not, she stopped whistling and heard the soft tattoo of loping hoofs. She turned, and there he was, half a furlong back and obviously meaning to overtake her.

She wondered if he had figured out from the sunbonnet that she was female. Was that why he was coming up so fast? No, I must look like something out of P.T. Barnum's Congress of Monsters, she thought. Maybe he hasn't figured out just *what* I am and is overwhelmed with curiosity.

She didn't glance back again until he was within a few yards. He was a big man, bearded, and his hat was pulled low so that the brim hid his eyes. He wore a dark coat, gray vest and trousers, black boots. He was rather well dressed, she thought, or would have been if he hadn't been so dusty. There was even dust on his beard. There was something familiar about him that she didn't pinpoint until he rode up beside her and matched his horse's pace to hers. He was riding Old Red.

He was giving her a hard looking over, and she was tempted to ask him if he saw anything green. She wasn't sure what that meant, except that it was sassy. She decided to be polite. "Nice morning," she said.

The man gave a little nod of his head and touched his hat brim. "I'll ride along for a little way, miss, if you don't mind. Where are you headed?"

"Langtown."

"Long ride."

"Yes, sir."

"Pretty horse you have there."

"It's my brother's. How come you're riding Old Red?"

"You know him?"

"I sure do."

"I traded for him at a ranch back there."

She was surprised that Mr. Snyder would trade Red and she said so, pointing out that the Snyders had raised him from a colt.

"Sometimes a trade comes along that a man just can't resist," the stranger said. He said it a little slyly, as if he didn't much care if she was suspicious or not. "My name is Jackson, ma'am. May I ask yours?"

"Dundee."

Mr. Jackson lifted his hat and she saw that he had rather large dark eyes and a head of curly hair with gray on the sides. Or maybe that was dust. Anyway he looked to be around forty years old. He seemed to have nice manners.

"You know, Mr.—uh, Snyder?" he asked.

"I've been living with him." She quickly added, "And Mrs. Snyder, of course. I was their hired girl, sort of."

He asked casual questions about the Snyders, Timbo, her parents. He had a friendly way about him, and she found herself chattering out her life story. She told him how Father had died when she was ten, leaving Mother with her and Timbo, a rocky little farm on Fool's creek, and a power of debts. Mother had hung onto the farm as long as she could.

Then she'd gone to work at the Sperrysville bakery, which was owned by Mrs. Snyder's cousin. She saw Timbo through high school and Laura Jean almost through before she died. Then Timbo got married, and Laura Jean moved in with the Snyders, where she worked for room and board. She'd been able to finish high school, walking a mile to the stage road every morning to meet the Steiner kids and riding the eight miles to town with them in their spring wagon. Evenings and weekends she cooked and did laundry and housework and such. Timbo had sent her three dollars a month, which was all the money she saw. It must have been a burden on him because he was trying to make it on a little ranch near Langtown with a baby on the way and two mortgages on his land and another on his livestock. Now she was going up there to live with him and help Sally with the baby and she had the promise of a job at the Blue Ribbon Home Cooking Restaurant in Langtown. She would be paid five dollars a week plus meals, and she could keep the tips that traveling men sometimes left!

She suddenly stopped talking, thinking that she was rattling on too much even if Mr. Jackson did seem to be genuinely interested. Well, the time did go faster if you talked. The river, scantily marked by a line of straggling green foliage, was less than a mile ahead now.

"I plan to save four dollars and fifty cents a week," she said. "Do you know how much that figures to in a year?"

Mr. Jackson hesitated hardly at all. "Two hundred and thirty-four dollars."

22

"Hey, you're good at figures."

"Don't do it," he said. "Spend it as fast as you make it. Spend it on pretty clothes. Some young rooster will come along and want to marry you."

"I don't think so."

"You don't want to get married?"

"Well, I've got a crazy idea in my head and I'm going to do it. I'm going to college."

He gave her another looking over. "You're dead set on it?"

"I know it's crazy. College isn't for girls, except rich girls. But I've been accepted at Montana State. I can't make it this September, but next year—"

"You'll have two hundred and thirty-four dollars."

"Plus what I save during the summer. If I can get a job for my room and board, I can make it on that."

"You'd better be dead set on it or you won't. The odds are against you, you know. Oh, you'll probably save the money. But your brother will need it, and you'll let him have it. And some young rooster will come along and you'll get married."

"No, sir. I'm dead set."

"Good. What do you plan to do, be a teacher?"

"I haven't made up my mind for sure."

They rode on a little way in silence. Then he said, "Look here, Miss Dundee. I didn't tell you the truth about this horse. I did trade for him in a way, but Mr. Snyder wasn't present."

"You just helped yourself?"

"I left a very good horse in his place."

Laura Jean experienced a twinge of fear. The man carried a rifle in a saddle boot slung under his right leg. There was a bulge on his right hip under his coat

23

that was surely a revolver. She had heard stories of cold-blooded killers who hid their viciousness behind a friendly manner.

"You see," he said, "I'm on the run."

"Oh. I'm sorry. I mean—"

"Mind you, I didn't say I'm running from the law. In fact, I will say flatly that I am not. The men after me have a grudge against me and want to kill me. An old family feud. It's important that I tell you that. Are you beginning to understand?"

"I don't think so."

"Do you know what an accessory after the fact is?"

"Yes, I guess so."

"Well, if you should decide to help me, I don't want you worrying about being an accessory after the fact. So I have told you clearly that it is *not* the law that is after me. You have no reason not to believe me. So—"

"Wait a minute. Help you?"

"Yes, ma'am. Trade horses with me."

"I don't think so."

"You haven't heard my offer yet."

"You told me you stole Old Red, Mr. Jackson. If I were to trade with you, that would certainly make me an accessory after the fact of horse theft. Or worse. And you'd have Flag and I'd have nothing because Old Red is the property of Mr. Snyder."

She stuck her chin in the air and angled away from him. The river was only a furlong away. He made the change of direction, too, and swung close to her—almost within touching distance.

"You're a sharp little fixin'," he said, grinning through his beard. "But you don't understand. I want to give you Red to return to Mr. Snyder. Then I propose to buy the mare from you."

"She belongs to my brother, not me."

"He wouldn't mind your selling her if you got an extra good price, would he?"

Flag was a pretty horse and a sound one but just a cowpony. She had a fairly smooth, ground-covering walk and a good canter, but her trot was so ragged as to be all but unridable. Timbo had paid thirty dollars for her.

"Fifty dollars?" Laura Jean said.

"Let's say sixty."

"Well, I guess—all right."

Mr. Jackson fished a folded paper from a vest pocket and waved it. "This is a bill of sale for the blue I left at the Snyder place. It's signed by the liveryman at Sperrysville. I'll sign it over to you."

"You're throwing him in?"

"He's for you. Call it a commission."

"Now wait a minute. There's a catch to this somewhere."

"Yes, ma'am. We'll change saddles when we reach the river. We'll ride into the water to do it."

"I don't know about that."

"There's no sense in changing at all if the men following can figure out from our tracks that we did it. You'll get your feet wet, Miss Dundee, but you may save my life. And I'm afraid there's another condition. I suppose you plan to cross the river and then turn north along the mountains to the stage road."

"Yes, I do."

"Well, I'm going to ask you to go a bit out of your way. I want you to turn south and ride in the river for

25

a way. Say half a mile. Then come out of the water, bear south and east, and swing around the end of that big butte. Then you can point north along the other side of the range.''

To the north, the War Bonnets bent westward and broadened into a tangle of interlocking mountains; but here they tapered off into an abrupt, single file of peaks. They were broken by a low saddle where the stage road crossed. They ended altogether a couple of miles south of here, culminating in a huge black butte with a bench at its foot.

''That'll take me ten miles out of my way!'' Laura Jean protested.

''More like six.''

''I could get lost.''

''I don't see how, Miss Dundee. All you have to do is head north along the other side of the mountains instead of this side. Stay close to them and you'll hit the stage road. It doesn't turn north till it's a mile or so beyond the range.''

The Saint Terry wound through a wide, low-banked bed, singing softly. At this time of year it was a scant fifty feet across and very shallow. At Mr. Jackson's insistence they separated as they approached the stream, leaving Flag's tracks to the north and Red's to the south. Once in the water, they turned toward each other, met on a shallow bar, and dismounted. Changing saddles here was a bit tricky, but the horses were in a tolerant mood, and they accomplished it without mishap.

Mr. Jackson produced a stubby pencil from a coat pocket, scribbled on the bill of sale he had promised, and handed it to Laura Jean. He stripped bank notes

26

from a roll and gave them to her, too. She looked them over carefully, not being used to paper money. They seemed genuine and she shoved them into a pocket of her overalls. He gave her a leg up on Red. He had very nice manners.

Riding south, staying in the water, she looked back and saw that he had crossed the stream and was riding north along the east bank—just as she had intended to do. The water was seldom more than a foot or two deep except for a few holes that she easily avoided. When she estimated that she had traveled half a mile, she reined onto the east bank and pointed southeast toward the bench at the foot of the butte.

Two and a half hours later the sun was high and hot. The bench crossing was well behind her and she was riding north again with the uneven wall of the range on her left. The stage road couldn't be more than a few miles ahead, she thought. Then she looked back and saw a great cloud of dust behind her.

IV

Mr. Jackson had given the impression that only a handful of men were after him—family feuders or whatever. It was disconcerting to see forty or fifty riders coming at her, spurring their horses and waving guns.

Whatever you do, Mr. Jackson had said, don't try to run from them or even look like you're thinking about it. Turn around and face them and wait.

It wasn't easy, but she puckered up and whistled "Onward Christian Soldiers" and watched them come on. As they drew close Old Red showed signs of nervousness. She tightened the reins, realizing that if he should bolt, she'd be shot out of the saddle in about two jumps.

The first riders curled past her and came up behind her. This put her in the center of a dust cloud as the others closed in. There was a long moment of confusion with ghostly figures weaving close and swinging away and yelling at one another. Then she was confronted by a wild-eyed little man whom she recognized as soon as he opened his mouth.

"You're the Dundee girl!" Sheriff Hornbill yelled.

"Yes, sir."

"Where do you think you're going?"

"North," she said.

He put a hand to his hear. "Speak up!"

"North!"

A heavy-set man worked his horse up beside Hornbill's. He touched his hat. "I'm Sheriff Briley of Hooper County. We seem to have misread your tracks."

"The Snyders said you'd be on a pinto mare!" Hornbill yelled. "You changed horses with somebody!"

"With Mr. Jackson."

"You know him?"

"I rode a way with him. He told me his name. We changed horses in the middle of the river."

"And you rode in the river like you was trying to hide your trail! And you come around this end of the range! Lord A'mighty, girl, you aided and abetted a fugitive from justice!"

"He told me he was a fugitive from an old family feud. Besides, I'm reporting to the law at the first opportunity, aren't I?"

"He force you to trade horses?"

"No, sir. He gave me Old Red to return to Mr. Snyder. Then he bought the mare from me for sixty dollars."

"He gave you cash money? . . . Coin or bills?"

"Bills."

"Let me see 'em."

She dug the bills out of her pocket. Hornbill pulled his horse close and she gave them to him.

"This here is stolen money, young lady. I got to

confiscate it."

"You can't—" Laura Jean protested hopelessly. "How do you know those particular bills were stolen?"

Briley extended a palm to Hornbill. "The crime took place in my county. If there's any confiscating, I'll do it."

Hornbill hesitated, then handed over the bills.

They went on questioning her, demanding details, Hornbill yelling and she yelling back. Briley was calmer and more to the point, but he had to yell, too, so Hornbill would hear him. Others crowded close to listen, their expressions grim and accusing, except for two or three riders who dozed in their saddles.

Finally, it was finished and the posse got moving again. There wasn't much it could do, Briley pointed out, but continue north to the road and look for tracks there. Many of the horses were near exhaustion, and the group traveled in a ragged, straggling line. Laura Jean trailed along. She rode alone at first, then Perry Raumbaugh and Pinky Greene came over and rode on either side of her.

Perry and Pinky were both about twenty years old and had reputations as girl chasers. They had never paid much attention to her before, but she was the only female within half a day's ride so now they were bent on making an impression.

They had been on spring roundup, hired temporarily by North American Land & Livestock, a multi-million-dollar corporation that had mining and cattle interests from here to Texas. They were full of big-outfit talk. They spoke of small ranchers like the Snyders as one-bucket outfits. Pinky was wearing a revolver, which he kept touching as if to make sure it was still there. Perry carried a shotgun across his saddle. Their horses were in comparatively good condition, and they were keeping tab on the others and commenting smugly on those that looked as if they wouldn't last much longer. They were counting on the posse dwindling down to just a few who would share in the reward.

Pretty soon they began to tease Laura Jean in a kind of fresh way. She didn't mind at first, even when they suggested that maybe she changed clothes with the fugitive as well as horses. But they went on from there to unfunny innuendos that she thought pretty tiresome. When she got a chance, she reined away from them and rode beside Sheriff Briley.

"You have sixty dollars that belongs to me," she said. "I'd like a receipt."

"No need for that." Briley produced the bills and passed them to her. "That Hornbill is a little excitable."

"Thank you. What did Mr. Jackson do—rob a bank?"

"He robbed a horse trader who posted a big reward for the recovery of his money."

"How much?"

"It reckons out to six hundred and ninety-eight dollars."

She let out a whistle that turned heads in their direction. "Could one person collect it *all?*"

"It's possible, not likely. We'll lose about half this party when we get to the stage road. Chances are the rest will split the money."

Em Foster jogged up on the other side of the

sheriff. Em was built like a mellon and must have weighed two hundred and fifty pounds. However, he was on a tall, big-boned horse that was holding up better than most. Laura Jean gathered that Em had been in the poker game where all the trouble had started.

"At first I took Jackson for some kind of business man," Em said. "A cattle buyer or maybe an accountant or something for North American Land & Livestock, something like that. The more I think about it, the more I figure him for a full-timer at the card table, a professional."

"Doesn't seem like a professional would go off half-cocked the way he did," Briley said, "but you may be right. How would you peg him, Laura Jean?"

"I don't know. He was kind of formal but real easy to talk to. Gosh, I told him practically my whole life story."

"He say anything that might be a clue as to where he came from or where he was going?"

"I don't think so."

"Think hard. Any little thing you can remember might help."

"He could do arithmetic in his head. He was real fast at it."

"An accountant?" Briley said. "Maybe an engineer?"

"Maybe."

"A card player," Em Foster said.

When they reached the stage road, Briley called a halt a few hundred feet short of it. He and Hornbill went ahead to study the ground and then waved the others forward. A wagon had been over the road in the last hour or so, but Flag's tracks could be picked out here and there. It looked as if Jackson was headed on up the road.

As Briley had predicted, almost half the possemen dropped out here, taking the road back across the range. The others trailed along the road, which ran eastward for a way before bending north. Less than a mile beyond the bend it crossed a bridge over a swift little creek with scrubby cottonwoods along its bank. Hornbill called a much needed rest here. Men got down from their saddles and clustered in the freckled shade, tying their horses so they wouldn't drink until they had cooled down a bit. Laura Jean dismounted, too, glad for a chance to stretch her legs.

Suddenly everyone was staring up the road at a great coil of dust that was racing toward them. At first Laura Jean thought it was made by a stagecoach; then she saw that it wasn't. There was a vehicle at its point but no horses. Before she could put a name to it, someone else did.

"Motor car!"

It was the first she had ever seen. She had heard that Mr. Lloyd Tackleman, the millionaire, had shipped one to Butte and had it at his lodge on Cipher Lake.

"Tackleman!" somebody said. "By God, we might have known."

The car slowed as it drew close, then it swung buckety-jump off the road and came to a stop. It was not much like the pictures of curved-dash Oldsmobiles and White steamers that Laura Jean had seen in magazines. It was a long and sporty-looking two-seater with the motor under an elongated hood in front of the driver and the radiator in front of that.

There was a wheel to steer by instead of a bar. Body and fenders were enameled a sleek green with a yellow stripe. Horn, headlights, and radiator were gleaming brass.

The two occupants stepped from either side of the vehicle as Sheriff Hornbill hurried along the bank to greet them. One was a brawny man in a linen duster and derby hat. The other, the driver, wore goggles under a long-billed hunting cap. He, too, wore a duster, which he immediately stripped off and tossed into the back seat. He then took off cap and goggles and dropped them into the car, too. He was in his early forties, clean shaven, and had neatly trimmed reddish hair that came to a sharp peak on his forehead to give him a rather dashing look.

"The man himself," somebody said. "The great hunter of dangerous game."

Laura Jean recognized him from a picture she had seen in *Cosmopolitan*. It had appeared with an article about Africa and had showed him sitting on a dead rhinoceros. Lloyd Tackleman, she thought as her fascination shifted from car to man. He controlled North American Land & Livestock, several western banks, and gosh knew what-all back East. He wasn't quite in the same class with J. P. Morgan or James J. Hill, but folks said he might be someday.

Sometimes, though, it seemed as if the ruling passion of his life was for hunting rather than finance. Here in Montana he killed bighorn sheep and grizzlies. He had stalked rhinoceros and such in Africa, tigers in India, Kodiak bear in the Aleutians. Since Cipher Lake was entirely surrounded by land that belonged to North American Land & Livestock, few local folk had seen his lodge there, but it was said to be a showplace of trophy horns, hides, and heads. And somewhere along the line Lloyd Tackleman had taken up pursuit of the craftiest and most dangerous animal of all. He had tried to quash publicity about it with only partial success, and it was an open secret. His favorite quarry was man.

Twice, Laura Jean remembered, he had joined the Pinkertons in Wyoming when they were trying to run down members of the notorious Hole-in-the-Wall gang. On another occasion he had come all the way from New York to take part in a month-long, two-state chase of a convicted killer who had escaped from Deer Lodge penitentiary. She had even heard it whispered that he had been a member of a firing squad in Utah, where shooting was the legal method of execution in capital cases. That was just a rumor, but he obviously had political influence that he used effectively at times. She recalled that a U.S. marshal had once publicly criticized him for "interfering" on a manhunt in Oklahoma Territory and then, promptly, had publicly apologized.

"Glad you could join us!" Hornbill bellowed as he and Tackleman shook hands.

"How are you, Sheriff? I appreciate your notifying me."

"Got a desper-ay-do loose right in your back yard! Be a shame not to let you know!" Hornbill seemed very pleased with himself. He must have telephoned to Table City and had word taken to Tackleman at his lodge, Laura Jean realized.

Led by Em Foster, men drifted up to look over the car. Em waddled up to the radiator, laid a hand on it, and took it off quick. He turned to the man in the derby.

"This looks like one that came all the way from Europe," Em said.

The man nodded.

"Germany?"

The man nodded again. Em turned to Tackleman.

"A Daimler?"

"Well, yes," Tackleman said pleasantly. "It was made by the Daimler people, but they don't call their machine by that name any more. They call it a Mercedes."

"How many cylinders?" Em was doing his best to appear knowledgeable.

"Four cylinders," Tackleman said. "Thirty-five horse power. The most powerful automobile in production."

"Auto—?"

"Automobile. A word the French invented."

Perry Rumbaugh and Pinky Greene stepped up to introduce themselves to Tackleman and tell him they had been working for his company during spring roundup. He shook hands and was cordial enough, but Hornbill looked annoyed. He touched Tackleman's elbow and led him over to where Sheriff Briley was seated at the foot of a cottonwood, writing in a composition book. Briley accepted Tackleman's handshake without getting to his feet.

"You meet anybody on the road?"

"Nobody," Tackleman said. "We came from the lodge, of course. We've been on the stage road for only about ten miles."

"By God, that means Jackson's more'n ten miles

ahead of us!" Hornbill barked.

"Or he's left the road," Briley said.

"If he stays in flat country, we ought to run him down quickly enough," Tackleman said. "You gentlemen riding with me?"

"I'll stay with the party," Briley said. He went back to writing in his book.

Hornbill got a Winchester and joined Tackleman at the car. Tackleman took a long, heavy rifle from the back seat and slipped a cartridge into the chamber.

"Sharps .50," he said. "Gun the buffalo hunters used. Still the best long range big-game rifle in the world. I knocked over a springbok with this one at a thousand yards."

"A what?" Perry Rumbaugh said.

"Don't show your ignorance," Pinky Greene said.

Hornbill got into the back of the Mercedes. Tackleman slid in behind the steering wheel and manipulated mysterious buttons and levers. The man in the derby, whose name was Hurley, cranked. When the motor caught, he took Tackleman's place at the wheel, and Tackleman got into the back seat with the sheriff. The car circled back to the road and rolled northward. The men in the back settled themselves regally, holding their rifles with stocks rested on the seat and muzzles pointed at the sky. Laura Jean watched the image disappear, erased by its own billowing wake.

"Au-to-mo-bile," she said softly to herself, savoring the word and the wonder and fixing them in her memory. "A Mercedes au-to-mo-bile."

She had two ham sandwiches carefully wrapped

and stowed away in the floppy duffel bag that was lashed behind her saddle. She got them and went over and sat down beside Sheriff Briley and insisted that he take one. Others threw them envious looks as they sat under the cottonwood and munched.

Briley continued to write in his book, and she asked about it. He said it was just a journal that he kept. "Keeps me from forgetting details," he said.

She stole a look over his shoulder and read a few lines:

"Candlestick Creek, Bannock County. Same day, 1:56 P.M.

"We cut a rusty and followed one L. J. Dundee, female, aged 17, instead of Jackson and went around the south end of the War Bonnets, losing an estimated 1 hour. It turned out she changed horses with him. The rational process of an unguided female in her teens can defy understanding. . . ."

V

The party continued along the road, Laura Jean with it. The road bore north northeast, rising a bit, winding among gentle outreachings of the burgeoning range to the west. White-faced cattle grazed on slopes, tails switching. Newly branded calves romped in spite of afternoon heat. A southbound stage appeared suddenly on a turn and came to a swaying stop. Briley asked the driver a few questions and it moved on.

Later, the riders reached a stage station. The keeper, alerted by Hornbill and Tackleman, had put his wife to making doughnuts and had about a bushel ready. He also had a big kettle of coffee, which most of the possemen laced with way-station whiskey or eschewed in favor of bottles of Gilbert's beer, chilled in the well. As they were pulling out of the station yard, the Mercedes pulled in.

"We been clean to Table City!" Hornbill yelled, standing in the car as riders kept a tight rein on frightened horses. "I had telephoned my deputy there and had him on the look out. Jackson didn't show up! The bugger left the road someplace; we ain't found where!''

They got on the move again. Briley led the way and the Mercedes brought up the rear. The car and the stage had hopelessly obliterated Jackson's tracks in the road, but Briley watched the edges. After a couple of miles, he spotted where the fugitive had left the road.

It was at an unlikely place where the road clung to a slope above the head of a long, narrow gulch. The grade was so steep as to be risky. It was decided to go back down the trail and find an easier way into the gulch. The Mercedes needed a wide area in which to turn around and there was none wide enough for some distance ahead. So it backed down the road.

At the foot of the hill a little ravine led into the gulch, and the horsemen trailed into it. The going was too rough for the car. Hornbill said they would take it to the other side of a sharp-rising little ridge that lay to the west. The gulch led through a break in the ridge to a flat valley, and they would meet the others there.

Laura Jean trailed along with the posse. She tried to keep out of Briley's sight, but he spotted her and dropped back beside her.

"Well, sis?"

"Howdy," she said.

"Why aren't you on that road and on your way to Table City?"

"I figure we'll head north the other side of that ridge. I might as well go that way."

"That kind of figuring will get you lost. Besides, this posse is no place for you."

"I figure if I'm along when you capture Mr.

Jackson, I'll claim a share of the reward."

"Come on now, sis."

"I gave you valuable information, didn't I?"

"You led us clean around Robin Hood's barn."

"I guess my rational process defies understanding."

Briley puffed his cheeks, looking as if he were about to splutter. He laughed softly instead. "I got a right to say that, sis. I raised three daughters."

"I sure could use the money."

"Well, you can forget about it. If we collect the reward, the posse will vote on how to divide it. I don't see them including you in."

In less than half an hour they reached the foot of the gulch and found themselves in a strip of flat country between the ridge and the War Bonnets. The Mercedes was waiting for them. Hurley's feet were sticking out from under it and tinkering sounds came from underneath. Hornbill and Tackleman were scouting around, trying to figure out Jackson's tracks.

The party dismounted and let the horses browse while Briley and Em Foster joined in the scouting. There were some prairie dog burrows nearby, and Laura Jean sat down where she could watch them. the little animals were scared now and out of sight, but she knew they'd be poking their heads up soon. Pinky and Perry joined her. Then Tackleman gave up scouting and came over and sat down nearby. He was carrying the big Sharps rifle.

"There are plenty of tracks," he said, "but they just circle around without going anywhere."

"He must've rode off a little ways and walked back and swept out his trail," Pinky Green said.

41

Tackleman nodded. "What we need is a tracker. An Indian. There's a good one up around Lang-town—Jim Smoke. I have a notion to send for him." His eyes kept going back to Laura Jean as if he didn't know quite what to make of her. She kept watching the prairie dog burrows. One of the prairie dogs was peeking out now.

"I heard of Jim Smoke," Pinky said. "They say he give up being an Injun."

"How do you do that?" Perry demanded.

"He took citizenship. They can do that if they can read and write and pass the test."

"That don't make him white, though," Perry persisted.

"I'll tell you something," Tackleman said. "Out on the trail color doesn't mean a thing. You hunt with a man, kill with him, and he's your brother."

Pinky squinted thoughtfully. "What about this jasper we're hunting? What's he?"

"If he gives us a good hunt, he's to be respected." Tackleman indulged in a small smile. "We'll kill him with respect."

"Kill him?"

"The good ones don't surrender easily."

Twenty-five yards away a little prairie dog had crept out of his hole. He stood on his hind legs, peering and sniffing, twitching with curiosity. He was a young one, not quite fully grown.

Tackleman followed Laura Jean's eyes. Silently, he pointed out the little animal to Pinky and Perry. Then he raised the big Sharps to his shoulder. Laura Jean's protest caught in her throat. He's just sighting, she told herself. He would just click the hammer on an empty chamber.

The gun roared angrily. The prairie dog was flung backward as if by a sudden gust of wind.

"Jesus!" Perry said. "You plumb evaporated him."

Tackleman lowered the rifle, his expression intense, eyes shining. Perry got up and got the carcass and brought it back, holding it by a foot. The big bullet had not left much but the head and the legs.

"Took the guts right out of him clean as a whistle," Perry said.

Tackleman took the carcass and inspected it. "Guts, ribs, spine, everything." He flung it back toward its burrow.

Laura Jean got up and went to the Mercedes, pretending to look it over. Prairie dogs are pests, she told herself. They eat anything that grows. Grass, weeds, flowers, vegetables, grain—anything. Some of their towns extend for miles and destroy the range. Wheat farmers poison them by the hundreds. Pests.

As she approached the car, Mr. Hurley crawled out from under it. He was bald as a board and had greasy fingermarks on his head. He had a screwdriver in one hand and a wrench in the other. Tackleman came over to consult with him.

"Brake shoe was loose," Hurley said. He put the tools into a box in the back of the car and put on his derby.

"It's fixed now?" Tackleman said.

Hurley nodded. Tackleman laid a hand lightly on the small of Laura Jean's back.

"Come on, young lady. Let's give her a spin. Try her out."

She allowed herself to be led around the car and assisted into the left-hand seat. Tackleman climbed in behind the wheel. Hurley cranked. The motor caught, the car vibrated expectantly and rocked forward. When they reached a flat stretch of ground, Tackleman accelerated. Laura Jean clutched her sunbonnet.

They drove straight up the valley, swerving to avoid brush. After about a mile they made a wide turn and headed back for a way. Then they came to a stop. Tackleman turned to look at her, bending a little so he could see around the sunbonnet. I haven't said a single word, she realized.

"I'm Lloyd Tackleman." He held out his hand. She took it nervously. He had very blue eyes and a nice white smile.

"I'm Laura Jean Dundee."

"Hornbill tells me you changed horses with this man called Jackson. What does he look like?"

She told him. He asked more questions and she answered them: how was Jackson armed? did he seem to know the country? what was she doing out here all by herself in the first place?

Pretty soon she found herself jabbering away just as she had to Mr. Jackson. Only it was different, too. He was a New York millionaire and a famous manhunter and she had never in her life spoken to anybody near that important. And here he was with his piercing blue eyes and with his arm along the back of the seat behind her and it was no wonder her rational process was discombobulated. In the distance she could see that Sheriff Briley had stopped looking for tracks and was sitting on a rock and seemed to be

44

looking in this direction. And that didn't help, either.

"You see," she heard herself saying, "I have this crazy idea about going to college. . . ."

Briley was aware that the car had come to a stop a quarter mile away and wondered why, but he wasn't really thinking about that. He was thinking about Jackson's tracks. The man had ridden in a circle, going over the same ground three or four times. Whichever way he had gone from there, he had walked back and swept out his tracks. He had done it patiently and expertly without leaving a trace that anybody had been able to find. It wasn't reasonable for him to take the time to do that for more than a hundred yards, though. And there was no place within that distance that he could have got to, no stream or stretch of rock where he would leave no tracks. There was only—well, there was the low ridge they had just come through. Its slope was steep and ragged with rimrock, but there were places where a rider might work his way up.

Briley got his horse and slowly made the climb. After brief scouting he found Jackson's trail along the summit, pointed north again.

He rode to a place where he could signal the party below, and he saw the Mercedes coming hell-to-split back down the gulch. He blinked and squinted hard, not being able to believe his eyes at first. But it was absogoddamnlutely true. That funny little filly in overalls and sunbonnet was driving.

Briley signalled with a shot from his revolver and

then waved his hat. While Hornbill and some others inched their way up the ridge, he watched Laura Jean get out of the car and walk over to her horse. Tackleman went with her and gave her a leg up.

About half the posse climbed the ridge. The others rode parallel along its foot, with Tackleman and Hurley leading the way in the car.

The ridge was a chain of summits with sharp ravines between them, and the going was slow. After a time the trackers reached a gap in the chain, a deep saddle with a cattle trail over it. The soil here was churned to powdery dust that was softly pocked by the hoofs of cattle and the horses of drovers, and Jackson's trail was indistinguishable. Briley finally found it again on the east side of the ridge. Reunited, the posse followed it over rolling country. The Mercedes chugged along, sometimes disappearing for long detours around gullies and sharp little rises.

Just before sundown they reached a wagon trace that led back over the ridge. Jackson had taken it and they followed it to a ramshackle house and a weather-beaten barn. Behind the barn, a creek wound through a large, green pasture where a black-and-white holstein cow and several saddle horses were grazing.

Laura Jean rode up beside Briley and Hornbill, pointing excitedly toward a horse in the pasture.

"That's Flag! The mare I traded to Mr. Jackson!"

A seedy-looking young man with uncombed blond hair came out of the house into the yard. A woman lingered in the doorway behind him. The man greeted Hornbill with a hesitant little salute.

"Sort of expected you, Sheriff. Feller was by about an hour ago. Looked like he was on the run."

"You give him a fresh horse!" Hornbill barked. "You aided and abetted—"

"You damn right bet I did! I was scared of him. He offered me a mighty fine trade and I took it."

"What kind of horse you trade him?"

"A rangy buckskin with a white blaze. Just a thirty-dollar cow pony. I would have took five dollars boot money and called it a fair deal, but he give me twenty dollars. Twenty dollars and the mare!"

"Which way'd he go?"

"West. Looked like he was headed straight into the mountains."

"An hour ago?"

"Thereabouts." The man gaped as the Mercedes bumped along the road and rolled into the yard. The woman came out of the doorway and stood on the porch, gaping, too.

The posse watered its horses at the creek and moved off, Briley and Hornbill leading the way. Jackson's trail led across the valley, angling a bit northward. The horses were tired and the posse was strung out for a hundred yards or so. Briley looked back and saw the Mercedes crawling along near the rear. Laura Jean was riding in the back seat. Her horse was tied to the car and was following along. And behind it—lead rope tied to its tail—was the pinto mare.

Briley reined up and waited.

"You buy back that mare, sis?"

"The man wanted thirty dollars," she said. "I got him down to twenty-eight."

Briley chuckled inwardly as he cantered back to the

head of the party. She'd got her brother's horse back for him, and she had thirty-two dollars and the bill of sale for a blue roan in her pocket.

The sun sank behind the War Bonnets, blackening their peaks, leaving a tattered crimson skirt of sky. Shadows thickened as the party reached the first claws of the range. The trail swung north and then turned into a steep-walled canyon.

Hornbill called a halt. When the Mercedes rolled up, he called to Tackleman.

"What do you say?"

As the car stopped, Tackleman stood up, looking into the canyon.

"I've hunted cougar in there, and it's a maze. Side canyons, brushy gulches."

"We can't track in there after dark!" Hornbill yelled.

"He's not going anywhere much after dark, either," Tackleman said. "Camp here. Set up a watch to make sure he doesn't try to sneak out of there. Then go in at first light."

Hornbill yelled to make camp. Laura Jean got out of the car and untied her horses. She led them toward Pinky and Perry, who had dismounted a few yards away. Briley reined over to intercept her.

"You're going to lay over at Andy Snyder's brother's place, aren't you, sis? You know your way there from here?"

"There's been a change of plans," she said. "I'm going to spend the night as the guest of Mr. and Mrs. Tackleman. I'm going to ask Pinky Greene to take care of my horses."

"Well now, sis," Briley said. "Whoa up. Seems like

the Snyders must be expecting you. Probably waiting dinner."

"Mr. Tackleman is going to get word to them. To my brother, Timbo, too. I'm going to work for Mr. Tackleman. Well, I think I am. We're going to talk about it tonight."

VI

Table City was a bleached little plateau town
sustained largely by memories of a booming frontier
past and hopeful rumors that the Northern Pacific
would someday build a spur in its direction. It had
geysered into life thirty years ago as a mining camp.
When the boomers boiled off, it managed to cling to
lukewarm solvency through the dubious largess of
one remaining silver mine on Gemini Ridge and as a
trading center for a cattle raising area.

Two weeks ago the mine had shut down. The
stunned reaction of the town was evident in the
number of unemployed miners in the saloons this
Sunday evening, trading talk of an early reopening,
signing chits, and blaming their misfortunes on
McKinley's reelection and the soullessness of con-
glomerates such as Cyclops-Umatilla—the parent
company of the Gemini Mining Corporation.

Even though most of Table City had seen the
Mercedes on various occasions, the saloon crowd
clustered at the batwings to watch it chatter down
Commerce Street. It came to a rocking halt in front of
one of the town's three brick buildings—the building

50

that housed a modest North American Land & Livestock office. Lloyd Tackleman and Hurley got out. So did a person in pants and sunbonnet, squintingly identified as probably female. It was known by this time that the millionaire was on another manhunt, right here in the county. Where did a girl fit into that? The manners and mores of the very rich would provide bar talk until closing time.

Hurley walked off toward the livery, where he meant to find somebody to take a message out to the ranch of Mr. Snyder's brother. Tackleman unlocked the door of the building and led the way up dimly lighted stairs to a hallway lined with doors. Laura Jean followed him past a dentist's office and a lawyer's office to a door with a frosted glass window with North American Land & Livestock lettered on it. He unlocked it and pulled a string that lighted a bulb under a green shade that dangled from the ceiling. Table City had a generating plant. It was also served by a telephone company that had a line south to Sperrysville and others all the way to Butte.

The office was large and shabby and plainly furnished. There were three desks, three chairs, one wooden filing cabinet. There was a typewriter on one of the desks, a telephone on another. Tackleman motioned to Laura Jean to sit at the third, on which there was an inkstand. He sat down at the telephone. After jiggling the hook awhile, he got central and gave the name of a man in Langtown. It took a few moments to make the connection. Then, speaking loudly, he gave instructions to hire Jim Smoke, the tracker.

"I want him ready to leave at once. I'm sending

51

Hurley with the car. I want him in camp by morning . . . Offer him whatever it takes. I'll fix it with Hornbill."

He hung up and turned to Laura Jean. "Why don't you write a note for Hurley to take to Langtown and send out to your brother?" When she hesitated, he went on persuasively, "Just tell him you're looking into the possibility of a job here and not to worry if you don't show up tomorrow. There's stationery in the desk there—second drawer, I think."

She opened the drawer and extracted a sheet of heavy bond paper with the words *Tenstone, Incorporated* printed at the top over a New York address. She took the pen from the inkstand, dipped it in the well. Tackleman got up, reached in front of her, and picked up the sheet of paper. He crumpled it and flung it into a wastebasket.

"My mistake," he said, smiling. "Wrong letterhead."

He got another sheet from another draw and laid it in front of her. This one bore the letterhead of North American Land & Livestock.

While she was writing, he made other telephone calls, jiggling the hook, speaking loudly into the mouthpiece of matters that she didn't understand. She quickly finished the note, found a matching envelope, addressed it.

There was a knock at the door. Tackleman nodded at her to answer it, and she admitted a thin, pale man in a business suit and bright red necktie. Tackleman quickly finished his call and stood up to greet the newcomer.

"Mr. Corner," he said, shaking hands. He nodded

52

toward Laura Jean. "This is Miss Dundee."

Mr. Corner gave her a curt nod. Amos Corner, she thought, president of the Table City bank.

"I saw your car downstairs," he said. "I've been trying to get in touch with you."

"I'm in a rush," Tackleman said pleasantly. "What can I do for you?"

"All Cyclops mines are shut down. Could you give me an idea when they'll reopen?"

"Me?"

"North American Land & Livestock has got control of Cyclops-Umatilla. I know that much."

Tackleman flashed his even smile. "I guess that cat's out of the bag. But I still can't give you a definite answer to your question. As a guess, I'd say most of the mines will be in operation in two months—including Gemini."

"I'm rather heavily invested in Cyclops stock."

Tackleman picked up his hunting cap from beside the telephone. He smoothed back his soft-looking red hair and put on the cap. "You or the bank?"

"Both."

"You've taken a beating."

"It's dropped twenty points in the last week or so. It's selling at four and a half now."

"And you want to know whether to hold on or sell. I don't give that kind of advice, Mr. Corner."

Tackleman flashed his smile again. Mr. Corner's expression was bleak.

"You're dead wrong," Corner said. "I'm not here to ask your advice. If the mines are going to reopen soon, the stock is a bargain. I'm in the market for more of it."

"All I can say is good luck. Cyclops has had some management problems. But you're right—we're in control now and we're putting in new people. You may be right about the stock. How much are you thinking of buying?"

"Maybe ten thousand."

Tackleman whistled through his teeth. "For a banker, Mr. Corner, you're a high roller. Just let me be clear. I make no recommendation one way or the other."

"Clear," Corner said. "There's one more thing I'd like to ask, though. There's a rumor that Cyclops is negotiating to sell mining leases to a company called Tenstone. Can you give me any information about that?"

"Tenstone?" Tackleman frowned and shook his head, distinctly giving the impression that he was not familiar with the name. "I've been away from New York for a month, Mr. Corner. I'm hardly an up-to-date source of information. Actually, Steve Gilly is more current than I am. He's here in the office every business day. Drop in and talk with him whenever you feel like it."

It was a dismissal and Corner muttered a somber thank you and left. A moment later Tackleman and Laura Jean followed him. Hurley was waiting in the car. Tackleman gave him Laura Jean's note with instructions to find someone in Langtown who would deliver it to Timbo's ranch in the morning. First, of course, he had to drive them to the lodge on Cipher Lake. Laura Jean rode in the back seat in a kind of bumpy dream as the Mercedes chased the ghostly splash of carbide headlights through the darkness. She tried not to think, accepting the unreality of the moment without challenge, and she found herself softly whistling a tune she couldn't put a name to.

The car turned into a side road and rolled on for several miles across almost level country. It slowed and stopped with its headlights on a big wooden gate. Tackleman got out, fit a key to a padlock, and swung the gate open. Back in the car, he explained to Laura Jean that North American Land & Livestock maintained a small herd of prize-winning Herefords here. Two full sections of land were fenced with barbed wire.

They passed the dark hulk of a barn, the dimly lighted windows of a bunkhouse, and a windmill. They pulled up beside a foreman's cottage and Hurley squeezed the horn. A man came out on the porch, a lamp in his hand. Tackleman joined him on the porch, and Laura Jean heard only snatches of his instructions.

". . . four men. Take the stage road and travel all night. You ought to be on the other side of the range by daylight. . . . Take extra horses. . . . Block the north pass. . . . Don't try to take him. Just drive him back. . . ."

As he came back to the car, he had an afterthought. "I'll want the dog. I'll pick him up in the morning."

A half mile farther along, the car made a sudden turn to the right and Laura Jean was aware of the lake on their left. Ahead, its lights glistening on the water, the lodge was set on a gentle knoll a few yards above the shore. As they drew close she saw that it was a huge two-story log building, deliberately rustic in design. There was a wide porch, colonnaded with logs, its roof a railed balcony. Both ran all the way around the building.

The car halted at porch steps marked by two coach lanterns. Laura Jean and Tackleman got out, and he reached into the back seat for his rifle and her duffel bag. Hurley drove off, the car disappearing around a corner of the building. Japanese lanterns hung from the porch ceiling, not lighted, rustling in the soft night breeze. A woman's touch, Laura Jean thought.

They went through a small hall into a very large room that took up about half the downstairs space. It was lighted by two chandeliers, circles of white-shaded kerosene lamps. There was a great stone fireplace at one end with a tiger's head mounted above the mantel. There were other animal heads all the way around the walls—moose, elk, bear, another tiger, a zebra. Fur rugs were scattered among heavy, rustic furniture.

Three people sat playing cards at a small table under one of the chandeliers—two women and a man. The man wore a white suit and the women wore white summer dresses.

"You're back," one of the women said. "Did you get him?"

"Not yet," Tackleman said. He put down Laura Jean's bag and opened the breech of the big buffalo gun. He extracted the cartridge and slipped it into a pocket of his hunting jacket. "Tomorrow, I should think."

56

"Well, you didn't come back empty handed," the woman said, eyeing Laura Jean. "What have we here?"

Tackleman performed introductions. The woman who had spoken was his wife. The other couple was Mr. and Mrs. Gilly. The women were in their early thirties. Mr. Gilly was a bit older—about Tackleman's age, Laura Jean thought—forty or whatever.

"Laura Jean is looking for a job," Tackleman said. "I thought we might use her at the office."

Mr. Gilly's eyebrows went up in a little show of surprise. Laura Jean tugged at the tie string of her bonnet. Instead of coming loose, it pulled into a messy knot.

"Steve—Mr. Gilly—is in charge of the office here," Tackleman explained. "If this works out, he'll be your boss."

"Can you use a typewriter?" Gilly asked.

"No, sir," Laura Jean admitted. "I guess I could learn, though."

"She could answer the phone, I guess," Gilly said unenthusiastically. "Keep the files straight."

"Do you live in Table City?" Mrs. Gilly asked.

"No, ma'am." The knot came untied and Laura Jean took off the sunbonnet. Her hair was surely a mess, she thought, and she desperately readjusted hairpins.

"She's from down near Sperrysville," Tackleman said. "We'll have to find a place for her to stay in town. Tonight she's our guest."

"How old are you, my dear?" Mrs. Tackleman asked.

"Seventeen."

"The office in town is open only when Mr. Tackleman is in this part of the country, you know."

"No, I didn't."

"So your job will be very temporary."

"We'll talk about all that later," Tackleman said reassuringly. "We'll work it out. Right now I'm starved. I'm sure Laura Jean is, too."

"Naturally, we didn't wait dinner," Mrs. Tackleman said. "Nancy, will you ask the cook to fix something? I'll show Laura Jean to her room."

"The south guest room," Tackleman said.

Mrs. Tackleman got to her feet, a tallish, quick-moving woman. "I think the little room off the south hall. She'll be more comfortable there."

"The south guest room," Tackleman said very slowly and emphatically.

Mrs. Tackleman shrugged elaborately. "Yes, sir, Mr. Tackleman, sir."

Laura Jean picked up her duffel bag and followed her up a staircase. Mrs. Tackleman started up the stairs swiftly and suddenly slowed, clinging to the rail. Then she moved swiftly again. Near the end of a hallway, she took a lamp from a wall bracket, opened a door, and led the way into a large room. There was a monstrous bed, a chiffonier, a smaller chest of drawers, and a dressing table. White fur rugs were strewn about the floor—polar bear, Laura Jean supposed.

Mrs. Tackleman put down the lamp. Cruelly, she ran her eyes the length of Laura Jean's overalls. "I was seventeen once, I really was. In fact, that was the year I met Lloyd." She crossed the room and opened a door that Laura Jean had supposed led to a closet. "Look here. This room has its own private bath."

Laura Jean caught her breath. She picked up the lamp and went in for a look. There was a water closet, a wash basin, and a huge tub. Big, velvety towels hung from racks.

"No electricity, no telephone," Mrs. Tackleman said, "but plumbing to spare. There are *five* bathrooms in this barn."

"Is there actually hot running water?"

"Actually. We have a two-hundred-gallon tank."

"I'm going to—would it be all right if I took a bath?"

"Splendid idea. How did you meet Lloyd?"

"It's kind of a long story."

"I bet it is. I thought he was on a *man*hunt."

As they moved out of the bathroom, Laura Jean got a whiff of Mrs. Tackleman's breath and the heavy sourness of alcohol. The lady was perhaps a little tipsy.

"He was," Laura Jean said. "So was I. That is, it sort of overtook me."

"Bless you. Why don't you just freshen up a bit and come downstairs? The cook will have some food ready. You can take your bath later."

She left the room. Ten minutes later, with some of the dust washed off and her hair combed, Laura Jean went back down. Mrs. Tackleman and Mrs. Gilly were sitting at the card table and sipping tall drinks with ice in them. Mrs. Tackleman smiled tightly.

"The men are in the dining room."

59

"Thank you." Laura Jean looked her in the eye and headed in that direction.

The dining room was a large alcove with windows that overlooked the lake. Gilly and Tackleman were seated at a table set with glistening silverware on a rich linen cloth. Tackleman was talking.

". . . just until Irene leaves for the East. Then—" He saw Laura Jean and got to his feet. "Come in, young lady. Sit here."

He pulled out a chair and seated her. The men were drinking beer. She had never tasted it, and Tackleman gave her a sip from his glass. A woman in a maid's cap came through a swinging door and set plates and bowls in front of her and Tackleman. A man in a starched white jacket brought a tureen and served thick soup with parsley floating on it.

"We stopped off at the office," Tackleman said to Gilly. "Amos Corner barged in on us."

"He's been pestering me," Gilly said. He took a cigarette from a silver case.

"He mentioned Tenstone."

"Yes, he's been trying to pump me about it. He picked up a rumor somewhere. I don't think he really believes it."

"I got the same impression," Tackleman said. "He's actually thinking of buying more Cyclops stock."

Gilly lit the cigarette. "He's already up to his ears in it."

"It might be a good idea for you to see him tomorrow. Play it right and you can unload ten thousand shares on him."

"Are we ready to unload?"

"Might as well cut North American's loss a bit. It will look good on paper."

"No danger of losing control of Cyclops?"

"In another two weeks the leases will be transferred. Control won't matter. And there's another angle to this."

"I think I see it," Gilly said. He glanced uneasily at Laura Jean. "The bank?"

"When Corner goes down, the bank will go with him."

"North American can bail it out, take it over."

"Another trout in the creek," Tackleman said.

The man in the starched coat reappeared with a large tray. Laura Jean had supposed there might be sandwiches or something like that at this late hour; but, he lifted covers from plates and there were thick cuts of tenderloin, au gratin potatoes, tender young carrots, sliced tomatoes, hot rolls. The final miracle was a scoop of ice cream with pineapple syrup. The lodge had an ice house, Tackleman explained. Stored in sawdust, ice cut from the lake in winter lasted all summer.

Tackleman told the waiter they'd have coffee in the other room. They found themselves alone there, and he sat beside her on a sofa with his arm along the back behind her.

"I've decided to arrange for a room for you at the Cattlemen's Hotel," he said. "It's just a block and a half from the office."

"A hotel? I can't—I don't see how I can afford that, Mr. Tackleman."

"North American owns the Cattlemen's. Room and board will go with the job." His fingers casually and very gently touched her shoulder. "As for your salary, what do you say to fifteen dollars a week?"

"A week?"

"Yes."

The offer was unbelievable. Whoever heard of a woman going to work in an office for the first time and earning fifteen dollars a week plus room and board? He couldn't be thinking of her as—well, maybe he could. There had to be a catch somewhere.

"And all I do is work in the office?"

"Eight to six, an hour for lunch. It will be pretty much of a grind, I expect, but I hope you can spend weekends here at the lodge."

"How long—I mean, Mrs. Tackleman said the office will close when you go back East."

"This year I expect it will be open at least until September. Steve Gilly will be here when I'm not."

"Well, it all sounds just fine."

"We'll be off before daylight, so maybe you'd better get some sleep now." His hand cupped her shoulder now, and he gave her a little hug. Then he was quickly on his feet. "I have things to do yet. I don't require as much sleep as most people."

"Good night." She got up and started for the stairs. Eleven weeks times fifteen dollars was a hundred and sixty-five dollars, plus thirty-two dollars in the pocket of her overalls plus a blue roan . . .

"By the way," Tackleman said. "You'll wear a dress in the morning, won't you?"

"Sure," she said.

There was a key in her bedroom door and she

locked it behind her. That was silly, she supposed, but she didn't want one of the servants barging in on her or anything like that. She drew a tub of steaming water, bathed with White Rose glycerine soap, used two of the huge velvety towels to dry off. She dug into the duffel bag for a nightgown and got into it. She turned down the lamp, blew it, and then drew back draperies from French doors that faced the lake. She opened them, stepped out on the balcony.

The water was only a few yards away, dark and smooth and making a sucking sound against a little pier that jutted into it. She found herself breathing deeply as if she could somehow take in this night and make it part of herself forever. Below her, a door scraped as someone stepped out on the porch. Then there were voices—Mrs. Tackleman's first.

"The moment you joined the posse, I knew this would happen. I didn't expect it quite so soon."

"My God, Irene," Tackleman said. "She's just a nice little girl who needs a job."

"They are always nice little girls, Lloyd. Children."

"You can stop it right now, Irene. Your imagination—"

"The nice little German girl in Africa. The nice little English girl in India—how old was she? Fifteen? And that nice little chambermaid in Colorado. She almost cost you some real money, didn't she? God knows how many nice little girls there have been!"

"There's not enough for you to do here," Tackleman said mildly. "So you sit around and imagine things. When you get back East, you'll feel better."

"Imagine things? My dear Lloyd, you're an open

book. Hunting, killing—you take to it as a drunkard takes to alcohol. The change in you is sharp and unmistakable. Among other things—shall I say it plainly?—it affects you sexually. When you go after big game, you get a girl into the scene every time you can. You want her to be there, to see you make the kill. If she hates it, I suppose that's so much the better. It makes her a little afraid, a little in awe of the rich, charming, and deadly Lloyd Tackleman."

There was a short silence with only the sucking sound of the lake against the pier. Then Tackleman said, "When you get back East, I want you to see that doctor again. The Swiss."

Mrs. Tackleman laughed thinly. "Lloyd, if you only knew!"

"He helped you."

"More than you know, my dear. Shall I tell you? It was the sessions with him that made me see you so clearly. Hunting. *Man*hunting. Girls . . ."

"You're twisting irrelevancies together, Irene. You're babbling."

"Innocence, killing, sex," she said. "It's a ritual. A sick ritual. You're the one who should see the doctor, Lloyd."

The pair strolled off the porch toward the lake, coming into Laura Jean's sight. If they turned, they would see her above them, and she drew back into the bedroom. She quietly closed the French doors. She found her way to the bed and sank into its soft embrace.

Irene Tackleman not only drinks, she thought, she is also slightly daffy. She's actually jealous of me. He was very patient with her. He thinks of me as a child, but that's kind of nice. Even if he doesn't *exactly* think of me that way, what difference does it make? He said definitely that he is going to pay me fifteen dollars a week, not a month. I'm going to live at a hotel and sometimes come here on weekends. I wonder when she plans to go back East . . . ?

VII

Fortified only by quick cups of coffee, they left the lodge before daylight. Tackleman, wearing duster, hunting cap, and goggles, drove. Laura Jean sat beside him. Gilly and Hurley rode in back along with guns, supplies, and two bright red five-gallon cans of gasoline. Hurley had been driving all night and was sleepy-eyed and unshaven.

At the foreman's cottage, they stopped and tooted the horn. An old man appeared from behind the cottage with a dog on a chain—a big, shaggy, snarling creature that had been trained to hate the human race. Hurley knew the animal and could handle him, so he took him into the back seat.

Darkness was thinning when they reached Table City. They pulled up in front of the Cattlemen's Hotel. Gilly, who lived here during the week, got out of the car. Laura Jean reached for her duffel bag and started to get out, too, but Tackleman laid a hand on her arm.

"Whoa. You wouldn't want to miss the excitement, would you?"

"I thought I was going to stay here," she said.

66

"You are. Steve will reserve a room for you, but we'll spend the day with the posse."

"But you said—" The car was moving off down the street. "I thought I was going to work in your office."

"Don't worry," Tackleman said. "You're on the payroll starting this morning. You can start at the office tomorrow or next day or whenever this manhunt is over."

Laura Jean tried to recall the conversation she had overheard last night. What had Mrs. Tackleman said? She'd accused him of wanting a girl on the scene when he made a kill. She had made it sound bizarre, and she had seemed a disturbed and jealous woman. Now it seemed as if there was some truth in what she said, after all. Well, what if there was?

"You even asked me to wear a dress," Laura Jean said.

Tackleman laughed, giving a little toss of his head. "I thought Irene might be up to see us off. She wouldn't approve of a woman on a posse. As far as she's concerned, you're at the office. Remember that."

"But Mr. Gilly—?"

"He understands. So does Hurley."

They reached the mouth of the canyon in dreary early light, with black shadows still fringing the camp. Bacon, eggs, hardtack, and coffee had been brought from Table City during the night, and the possemen were cooking breakfast. There was a scarcity of cooking utensils, and some of the men were cooking bacon on sticks.

Sheriff Briley sat beside a fire, writing in his composition book. When the Mercedes pulled up, he got to his feet. He seemed about to come over and speak to Laura Jean or Tackleman and then to change his mind.

Some of the men gathered around the car, keeping their distance as Hurley got out with the dog, which was snarling and straining at his chain. Tackleman took the chain from Hurley, keeping a short hold. When he stroked the dog's head, the dog growled deep in his throat.

"Hey, there, Apache," Tackleman said. "You don't growl at me, boy. I'm your boss."

Hurley was in front of the car, extinguishing the headlights. "He don't like to be petted," he said softly.

Tackleman laughed happily. "See that, boys? He doesn't trust anybody, not even me. He's a killer. Trained to it."

"What kind of dog is he?" Perry Rumbaugh asked.

"He's got some mastiff in him and some wolf-hound."

"Maybe a little wolf, too?"

"Maybe." Tackleman laughed again.

Sheriff Hornbill bustled up as if he were going to shake hands with Tackleman, but he took a hard look at Apache and stopped short. "Can he follow a scent?" he yelled.

"He's had some training in that direction," Tackleman said. "I don't know how good he is at it. But that doesn't matter much. We've got the best Indian tracker in the whole Northwest, haven't we? Where's Jim Smoke?"

"Present." The Indian was seated near Briley, eating bacon and eggs from an army mess kit.

68

"Come over here," Tackleman said. "I want you to meet Apache."

Jim Smoke looked up briefly and went back to his breakfast. "I'll meet the son of a bitch from over here."

Tackleman joined in the laughter. "Damn it, Jim, come here. You two are going to be a team."

"What two?"

"You and this dog."

Jim gave the dog a narrow look and made no other reply. He was well known in the county and Laura Jean recalled some of the things she had heard about him—mostly from Timbo. His ranch was near Timbo's. He had left the Blackfoot reservation, got citizenship papers, and taken out a homestead claim. There had been a legal hassle about an Indian's right to do that, even if he was a citizen. For a wonder, Jim had won a court battle. For another, he was accepted by his neighbors. He paid his taxes, sent his kids to school, got haircuts in the Langtown barber shop.

"I mean it," Tackleman said. "Look here. This dog could save your life. Suppose you close in on Jackson suddenly. He's behind cover and about to shoot you. What do you do? You let the dog loose. He'll go in fast and won't stop for anything. Even if Jackson should wound him, he'll keep going and tear the man to pieces. Damn it, come here."

Jim stuffed the last of his breakfast into his mouth and chased it with a gulp of coffee from a tin cup. He got to his feet and walked toward the dog, a heavy-set man with a round, cheerful face. He stopped six feet away. The dog strained at his chain, lip curled.

"Don't be scared of him," Tackleman said.

"You're jumping-A right I'm scared of him."

"Look what we've got here, boys," Tackleman said. "A famous, expensive, Indian tracker who's scared of a dog."

"My price just went up." Jim moved a step closer. The dog lunged for him, but Tackleman had a solid hold on the chain. "Jesus! He thinks I'm his breakfast."

"Let him see you're a friend," Tackleman said. "Just stand there and talk to me in a natural way."

"Nice day if it don't rain. And I got no use for a dog. If Jackson was afoot, it might be different."

"We'll take a walk together, get him used to you."

They walked out of camp, Jim keeping his distance at first. The dog decided they were hunting, looking for something for him to kill. He lost interest in Jim, who moved closer. When they came back, Jim was holding the chain.

"See?" Tackleman said. "That's a smart dog. I wouldn't take a thousand dollars for that dog."

The posse gathered around Tackleman and Hornbill for instructions. Tackleman did the talking with Hornbill nodding his agreement and now and then yelling a comment.

"This canyon branches into three or four, not counting little blind canyons," Tackleman said. "The southernmost has a climbable slope at its head. Jackson could work his way up that and double back down into this valley. But if he knows the country well, his best bet is to head northwest. There's a pass up there somewhere that will take him clear over the range.

"What he doesn't know is that I sent my foreman and four hands around to the other side of the range last night. They took the stage road and traveled all night. The pass is more accessible from the west side; so they ought to reach the summit before Jackson can from this side. If he goes that way, they'll drive him back down toward us and we'll have him trapped.

"Now there's another possibility. He may be more or less lost. We know he's good at putting down false trails, sweeping out his tracks, and that sort of thing. He may wind around in and out of canyons and try to get behind us. We'll leave a few men here so he can't get out this way. And we'll divide the rest of the posse into teams of two or three men each and follow every route that he might take.

"This is important. If you sight him, try to pin him down but don't try to take him. Signal with three spaced shots every five minutes and wait for assistance."

Briley elbowed his way through the group until he was squarely in front of Tackleman.

"Did Sheriff Hornbill tell you that a deputy from my county arrived here about an hour ago with some news? . . . Sam Swanson has regained consciousness. He's the hotel clerk that was slugged. He is rational and on his feet. So Jackson is not wanted for murder. I want him taken alive if possible."

"Of course," Tackleman said. "If possible."

"On the other hand," Hornbill yelled, "God knows what he's wanted for in other parts of the country! This is a desper-ay-do we're after! I don't ask nobody to spare his life at the slightest risk to the life

71

of anybody in this posse! Not the slightest!"

"I want him alive," Briley said steadily.

He went back to the fire and sat down, picking up his composition book. Tackleman began to divide the men into small teams, giving detailed instructions to each.

VIII

The Journal of Patrick H. Briley, Sheriff of Hooper County, Montana.

Cobweb Canyon, Bannock County, Monday, June 10, 1901, 6:05 A.M.

Deputy H. Kurtz arrived with news that Samuel Swanson, hotel clerk, is recovering from a blow on the head. Also reported that Yates, victim of the crime, sold off his string of horses at auction yesterday and headed north, supposedly for Table City.

Tackleman showed up a few minutes ago in motor car. The Dundee girl is with him. Allegedly she spent the night with him and his wife at the lodge on Cipher Lake.

I have been trying to piece together a mental picture of Jackson without much success. The man doesn't quite add up. He was cool and self-controlled during the card game and then blew up all of a sudden. An explanation would be that he took on a power of liquor during the game and it hit him all at once, but I am not sure that was the case.

In any case, he is no green pea. He knows how to

handle himself on the trail. I have a feeling we haven't seen all his tricks yet.

Tackleman has set up the chase so that he personally can make the kill. He does intend to kill. Since this is a personal journal I will state my opinion of a fellow law officer, a thing I wouldn't do in an official report. Harry Hornbill is at best a bright dullard. He is in awe of Tackleman and has given him free rein.

I have no authority here. I can't even pull out the Hooper County of this posse, because Hornbill redeputized them. They are under his command, and I am puckerstoppled.

I am planning to ride into Table City in the company of Deputy Kurtz, who will go back to Hooper. I am in need of a barbershop, hot towels, and a chance to think.

IX

The man called Jackson stood on a patch of scrub pine and watched the party below move past him, pointed south along the trail he had laid down last night. They were less than a mile away by trigonometry but four or five by the time they followed his crooked trace over the hogback to the south and then back up here.

There were six of them—five riders following a tracker who was on foot and who held a dog on a leash. The riders were keeping about fifty yards behind the tracker. One of them was a woman. The Dundee girl, Jackson guessed, though her presence made no sense to him now. She was wearing a dress today and she was riding the pinto—she must have bought it back from that homesteader. The man in the hunting cap was riding beside her.

Twice yesterday Jackson had studied his pursuers from a distance. He knew about how many there were, about how many horses were wearing down. He knew about the Mercedes. He knew who the man in the hunting cap almost certainly had to be, and he knew how dangerous he was.

What bothered him now was that there were only these six actually following his trail. That meant that the posse had split up and scattered. He had tangled his sign in the brush on the other side of the hogback. He had walked back and swept out tracks that would betray his true direction. He had taken great pains at it, doing exactly as a Crow warrior had taught him in his youth. He had counted on the trick delaying his pursuers for a time, maybe an hour. But he hadn't counted on small groups scouting the slopes and canyons to the north. And he hadn't counted on the dog.

Usually, a dog wouldn't be used to track a man on horseback. The only scent for it to follow would be that of a horse—which left a plain trail anyway. This dog, then, was perhaps more killer than tracker. Still, it might be of good service when it got to the place where he had covered his tracks. The scent would still be there—with man scent, too. The dog, if it was any good, would not be fooled.

Jackson's plan was simple enough. Get the posse tangled up in this mess of canyons and slip over the pass. The pass was high, hard to find from this side of the range, and seldom used; a stranger wouldn't be expected to know that it was even there. By the time the posse realized what he was up to, it would be too late to send horsemen around by the stage road to intercept him on the other side. They would try it with the car, no doubt, but that bothered him not at all. He had a suitable consequence planned for that Mercedes.

Something drew his attention to the tracker and the dog. Holding his hat in front of him to shade his eyes, he saw that the dog was pulling the tracker along faster than he wanted to travel. When the man came down on his heels and pulled the animal to its hind legs, it turned toward him angrily and was difficult to control. The man tried for a shorter hold on the chain. The dog spun, going for the man's arm. The man dropped the chain. The dog whirled back to the trail and raced on, free except for the dragging chain.

The horsemen galloped after it, but it reached the hogback well ahead of them. It was faster than a horse on the steep slope. The horsemen slowed, gave up the chase.

Without men to control it, there was no telling what the dog might do. It could be distracted by a rabbit or other small animal. It could wear itself out, drink too much and get water sick when it reached a creek. Or it could stay on the trail and catch up with Jackson in a hurry. If that happened, he would probably have to shoot it and risk giving his position away.

He turned into the pines where his horse was tethered, a tall buckskin he had got from the homesteader. "Time to absquatulate," he said whimsically and pulled himself into the saddle. He reined out of the trees and headed northwest.

He wound deeper and higher into the ragged, rocky range, staying in the shelter of ravines, avoiding summits except when he needed to scan the country ahead. He kept an eye on his back trail, too, thinking of the dog, visualizing it leaping over his horse's rump to attack him without warning.

He pointed for a saddle between rocky peaks,

climbed it, and then threaded through a series of sharp ravines that took him to the summit of the pass. This was a mile-long valley streaked with stands of brush and cut by draws. As he neared its eastern end, the valley narrowed, terminating in a little canyon just ahead. About a furlong away from the entrance to the canyon, he crossed a shallow draw, reining to the right as he rode out of it. A shot rang out from the canyon. His horse reared and fell.

As he threw himself from the saddle, there were more shots, a volley of them. Bullets kicked up dust and cut through brush on either side of him. The horse immediately got to its feet. Jackson rolled, caught the reins, and led the animal into the draw.

There was a deep, bloody gash high on the horse's chest. Chest muscles were torn, but the bullet had not entered the chest. The buckskin could stand. It could walk. Jackson led it back down the draw.

Firing continued, spaced now, although the shooters couldn't see him. Covering fire, he thought, calculated to pin him down. There were four or five men firing. There must be others circling, closing in on him.

He climbed the bank and peered through brush, studying the valley right and left. Except for spots of brush, the area between him and the canyon was clear. He watched for movement and saw none.

The firing was coming from the canyon, with the ambushers well concealed. They spotted him now and two of them fired at once, neither bullet coming really close. They weren't trying to hit him, he decided as he slid back into the draw. If they were, at

78

two hundred yards, he would be dead. They had shot his horse and were now just trying to pin him down.

Puzzled, he led the horse down the draw, which angled southeastward for a way and then bent sharply eastward to take him back in the direction he had come. The firing continued, apparently aimed at the spot where he had last been seen. He had another look over the edge of the draw and saw two horsemen now, riding close to the valley wall to the south. It was plain that they meant to circle him and cut off his escape back down the valley.

They were riding hard, headed for a long, low spur that reached down into the valley. If they could get behind that, they could work their way to high ground and good cover, but for a minute or two they were exposed. They probably didn't realize that he had come so far down the draw and that they would pass less than a hundred and fifty yards from him. He slid down, snatched his Winchester from its boot, scambled up the side of the draw again. He shot the first horse, dropping it with a head shot and giving the rider a bad fall. The second rider came to a skidding stop, threw himself from the saddle, and ran toward his companion. Jackson killed the second horse and slid back into the draw.

He led the buckskin to a place where the draw deepened and then he eased himself into the saddle. The horse moved stiffly and seemed in kind of a daze, but it did not limp. He patted its withers.

"There's not much I can do for you, old soldier," he said. "There's a great deal you can do for me. Take me as far as you can. Get me out of this trap."

It was crazy, he thought. Why hadn't they let him

reach the canyon, ride right into their ambush? He looked back toward the canyon and began to understand. A slender column of smoke rose from the canyon. A signal—its meaning as crisp as semaphore. It told the possemen below that he was here, that he had tried to go over the pass.

He had been thoroughly outguessed. Those men could have got here ahead of him only by traveling last night. They could not have made their way up the broken, trailless eastern approach in the dark, however. They had been sent by stage road to the other side of the range and the easier climb from there.

They were disciplined men, he concluded, and they were following strict orders. They were not to take him. They were to set him afoot, if they could, keep the pass blocked, signal. He was being hunted as a trophy animal is hunted, with an entourage of scouts and beaters to maneuver the prey into the sights of the privileged hunter who would make the kill. Jackson laughed softly.

"Can't plan much ahead now," he told the buckskin. "We've got to get out of this valley. After that we'll still be in a net, but it will be a loose net. There'll be holes in it. Do the best you can for me, old soldier."

He got out of the draw and urged the horse into an easy canter. He reached the foot of the valley and entered the first of the series of ravines below it. Escape depended on his getting through them before possemen, guided by the smoke signal, reached them from the other direction. He could make it, he guessed, if the horse held up.

He rode the slopes, keeping as far as possible from his previous course along the bottoms. The farther pursuers were drawn toward the pass before they discovered he had doubled back, the better.

The buckskin was breathing noisily, stumbling occasionally. Jackson dismounted and led the animal through the last ravine. With that behind him, he took a ragged course over unlikely ground that was hard on the horse. He reached a creek and turned down it, walking in the water. The horse was staggering badly. After a quarter of a mile it collapsed on the bank.

Jackson removed gear, worked the saddle free. He slipped a derringer from a clip holster in his left sleeve. It would be a bit less noisy than his Colt, and it would be just as instantly fatal if the shot was placed in the proper spot. Then, free of saddle, the horse struggled to get up.

Jackson seized the reins, helped the animal to its feet. He examined the wound again, washed it, plastered it with clay to keep the flies off. The horse was feverish, glassy-eyed. But there was water here and a little browse; perhaps it had a chance to survive. Jackson slipped off the bridle, picked up rifle, saddlebags, and canteen, and set off afoot.

He walked in the shallow creek, going back the way he had come until he reached a great slab of bedrock. He left the creek here, walking backward across the rock, bending, wiping his wet tracks away with a bandanna so that no faint outline would be left when they dried. He moved off at a sharp angle to the creek then, walking on rock when he could and making sure to erase tracks he left on softer ground.

He got over a rise and into the pinched upper end of a canyon with a steep but climbable hill above it to the south. There was timber at the top of the hill. It was a place to hole up until dark.

He made the long, slow climb to the top and paused to get his breath. The other side of the hill sloped away gently into the tangled country to the south. He studied the lay of it for a time, fixing landmarks in his memory.

He turned toward the trees, catching their cool coniferous fragrance and looking forward to a rest. As he neared them, three men appeared suddenly, and he was looking into two revolvers and a shotgun. He dropped his rifle and gear, raising his hands to the level of his head, taking care not to let his sleeve slide above the wrist holster. He tried a wild, desperate bluff.

"Take it easy, boys. My name is Owens. I just joined the posse this morning."

"Bullshit," Perry Rumbaugh said.

"You're Jackson," Pinky Greene said.

"Hey," Jackson said. "You're making a mistake."

"He fits the description," Al Schrockenmeyer said.

"Search him," Perry said.

Pinky stepped forward and snatched Jackson's Colt from its holster. Schrockenmeyer picked up Jackson's saddlebags and began to go through them. Perry stood back a few steps, his shotgun leveled. He laughed softly.

"I told you boys. Just find a nice shady place and

rest ourselves, I said. We'll do just as good as we will pounding out butts up one canyon and down the next."

"He walked right into our parlor," Pinky said, cautiously patting Jackson's pockets. He extracted a wallet, a poke with its drawstring wrapped around it, a number of cigars. He counted the money in the poke and the wallet. "He's got no more'n two hundred dollars here. I reckon the rest is in them saddlebags."

Schrockenmeyer was a tall, slow-moving, scowling man. "I don't see no money at all in here."

"See if he's wearing a money belt," Perry said.

Pinky unbuttoned Jackson's vest and shirt and pulled his shirttails out. He was wearing no money belt.

Schrockenmeyer had emptied the saddlebags on the ground. He dropped them on top of their contents. "Must be in his boots."

"Gentlemen, I tell you I'm not Jackson. How could I have his money?"

"Shut up," Perry said. "Sit down. Shuck off those boots."

Jackson sat down. He extended one leg and then the other, and Pinky pulled off his boots. "No money in here."

Perry walked up close. He touched the double muzzle of the shotgun against Jackson's bare midriff. He slowly and deliberately slid it down to the groin.

"I'm going to ask you just once. What did you do with the money?"

Jackson looked into the pinched young face and

thought that Perry was capable of shooting. Even if he didn't shoot, even if he came down hard with the muzzle of the gun, that would be almost as bad.

"All right," Jackson said. "I'm Jackson. I stashed the money."

"Where?"

"South of here a way. A couple of miles."

"You come from the north," Perry said. "We watched you climb the hill."

"Sure. I tried to get over the pass. It was blocked. My horse was shot. I turned back."

"Maybe he's telling the truth," Pinky said. "Remember? We thought we heard shooting."

Perry was uncertain. He stepped back, pointing the shotgun at Jackson's head. "We just as soon take you in dead. If you're lying, that's the way we'll do it."

"And leave all that money to rot?" Jackson reached for his boots. The edge of the wristlet to which the derringer was clipped showed beneath his sleeve, but nobody noticed. "Tell me, is there a reward posted for me?"

"Twenty per cent."

Jackson laughed. "Seems like I'm not much good without the money."

"Oh, you're going to take us to the money," Perry said. He lowered the shotgun significantly.

"How many left in the posse?" Jackson said. "Eighteen or twenty? Twenty per cent divided twenty ways. It won't come to a whole lot."

Pinky and Perry exchanged a sober look. Schrockenmeyer scowled. They were all thinking the same thing, Jackson guessed.

"Seems like it might be a time for a deal," he said.

They were unsure, suspicious. Two happy-go-lucky cowpokes and a hard-scrabble rancher, Jackson thought. Any one of them might shoot him if he had the slightest excuse, and he was careful to keep his coat sleeve tight against his leg as he pulled on his boots.

"What deal?" Perry said.

"There's close to thirty-five hundred dollars, all told. I'll take you to it. You keep the money, let me go. Who'll ever know?"

"Don't listen to him," Schrockenmeyer said. "I don't think we should listen to him."

"Gentlemen," Jackson said. "It won't hurt to talk. Sit down and let's talk about it."

"I can talk standing up," Perry said.

"All I want now is to get clear," Jackson said. "Give me your word, and I'll lead you straight to the money."

Pinky and Perry exchanged another look, a long one. Then they looked at Schrockenmeyer. They were thinking they didn't have to let him go, Jackson knew. Once they had the money they could kill him. It wouldn't be hard to hide his body where it wouldn't be found. From their point of view, that would be preferable to the risk of his being eventually caught.

"There's thirty-five hundred?" Pinky said.

"Around that."

"Schrockenmeyer?" Perry said. "What do you say?"

Schrockenmeyer spat. Then he bobbed his head suddenly and decisively. "I'll get the horses."

He turned into the trees and came back leading three horses. He took a lariat from a saddle and slipped the noose over Jackson's neck.

"You walk ahead of my horse. You try any tricks, I'll jerk your head off."

X

Briley came out of the barbershop freshly shaved, hot-toweled, and smelling of witch hazel. He bought cigars at the general store, lighted one, and headed for the hotel. Deputy Kurtz, who was on his way back to Hooper County, had said he believed Yates was here in Table City. If so, Briley wanted to talk to him.

The Cattlemen's was better kept than most Montana hostelries in towns not on a railroad. The lobby had a green carpet, comfortable chairs upholstered in leather, polished cuspidors, and a large plate glass window that provided a clear view of the street. The desk clerk was mustached and bespectacled and looked like Vice President Roosevelt. He watched with silent interest as Briley examined the register.

"This one," Briley said, pointing to Yates's scrawled signature. "He in?"

"No, sir."

"When did he check in?"

"Late last night."

"This name below his—Laura Jean Dundee. She stayed here last night?"

"No, sir. I wasn't on duty, but I understand Mr.

Gilly took the room for her and signed her in early this morning."

"Gilly?"

"A North American Land & Livestock executive. I understand Miss Dundee is an employee of the company."

"She's going to live here at the hotel?"

"Apparently so." The clerk suddenly pointed toward the plate glass window. "I believe that's Mr. Yates now, sir. Coming out of the bank."

Briley strode to the door and called. Yates turned briskly, a pot-bellied man wearing a white hat, white vest, and rumpled black suit with the empty right sleeve tucked into the coat pocket.

"I hear you got the thief trapped in the mountains," he said as they met. "I appreciate the effort you and all those good citizens are making."

They went into the hotel lobby and sank into chairs that faced the big window. It wasn't yet noon, but Yates smelled of whiskey.

"The hotel clerk came to," Briley said. "They say he's all right."

"I heard that."

"According to my deputy, he's kind of hazy and mixed up about what happened."

"Understandable."

"He told the deputy that Jackson came a-roaring into the hotel and asked what room you were in. He told him. Then he heard Jackson kicking in your door, and he got a gun and went up. He says he bumped into you as he entered the doorway. That's about all he remembers for sure."

"That's about the way it was," Yates said. "I was

trying to get away from Jackson. He was like a madman. I was afraid he'd kill me. But I bumped into the clerk. He was knocked off balance, and Jackson had the drop on both of us. He slugged the clerk and pitched me through the window."

"You feeling all right?"

"Hardly a bruise. I fall like a cat."

"Were you maybe a little drunk?"

"Maybe I was. Maybe that helped me to land relaxed."

"Mr. Yates, was there a fourth person in that room?"

"No, sir." Yates bit the end off a stogie and spat it toward a cuspidor. "Why do you ask that?"

"Swanson—the clerk—seems to have the idea that somebody followed him into the room or maybe came from behind the door and slugged him."

Yates gave a little shake of his head. "Jackson slugged him."

"Then he took your money from you?"

"He already had the money." Yates lighted his stogie. "He beaned the clerk and dragged me to the window and pushed me through it."

"Tell me," Briley said. "Had you and Jackson ever met before?"

"Just over cards."

"I mean before you came to Hooper County. Maybe a long time ago."

"No, sir. I travel a lot, meet a lot of people. But if I ever met Jackson, I sure don't remember him."

"Where was your hostler the night you were robbed? The Frenchy."

"With the horses, as usual. What are you trying to

get at, Briley?"

"I don't rightly know, Mr. Yates." Briley's cigar had gone out. He exploded a match with a thumbnail and relighted it. "That was an unusual robbery. The way Jackson acted doesn't make much sense."

"The man was like a lunatic. He came storming in like a Texas cyclone."

"Seems to me that during the card game you were wearing a gun in a shoulder holster."

Yates opened his coat on the armless side to display a shoulder harness and a holstered revolver. "I generally carry it."

"You had it on when Jackson robbed you?"

Yates nodded. "No chance to use it. He busted in with a big Colt in his hand."

"And Swanson had a gun?"

"Yes, sir."

"And Jackson was crazy mad?"

"Like a lunatic."

Briley puffed his cigar, staring thoughtfully through the window at the bank across the street. He tried to visualize the robbery and couldn't. There was something wrong with the story he was getting—maybe everything was wrong with it. He said, "It's a wonder he didn't shoot the clerk."

"It is."

"Instead he took the risk of getting shot himself and brained him. Doesn't seem like a man in a storming rage would do that. He'd shoot. Mr. Yates, what are you doing in Table City?"

"Wanted to be close to the posse. I appreciate what those good citizens are doing and—"

"What were you doing in the bank?"

Yates sighed noisily. He blew a scrap of tobacco from his lip. "I auctioned off my horses yesterday. I paid off the Frenchman and still had a little wad of cash. After what happened, I was uneasy about carrying it around. I made a deposit."

A stage pulled up in front of the hotel, discharging passengers and luggage. One of the passengers stood in front of the hotel window, staring in. He grinned and hurried into the lobby, extending his hand to Yates.

"By God, it's old Nowhere Yates! You should live so long!"

"Hello, Denny." Yates got to his feet and took the man's hand gingerly in his left. "Meet Sheriff Briley. Denny Wales."

"Wales," Briley said, placing the name as he shook hands. "Let's see. The agitator?"

"Agitator is one of the milder terms they apply to me." Wales grinned, a square-faced man with wild blue eyes and a missing front tooth. "More often it's anarchist—and worse."

He pulled up a chair and they all sat down, making a little circle in front of the window. Wales produced a sack of Bull Durham and began to roll a brown-paper cigarette.

"By God," he said, "I'm beginning to put it together. I heard there was a crime down here and a manhunt on. A one-armed man was robbed, they say. And here's old Nowhere Yates talking to a lawman. It was you?"

"It was," Yates said.

"They haven't caught the miscreant yet?"

"Not yet." Yates seemed eager to change the

subject. "And what brings you to these parts? The mine?"

"The mine indeed. The layoff gives an agitator a fine opportunity to agitate."

"A losing game," Briley said.

Wales chuckled. "I'm just twenty years ahead of my time. Me and Eugene V. Debs."

"Even the working people are against you most of the time," Briley said. "If you do make any progress with them, the bosses turn their bully boys loose."

"More often," Wales said pointedly, "the law does their dirty work for them. But you're right, it's a losing game. Sometimes I wonder why I do it."

A long-legged, towheaded boy came into the lobby. Yates got to his feet.

"I been looking for you, Mr. Yates," the boy said. "Wagon's about loaded."

"All right, son," Yates said. "I'll be right there."

"We packed the beer in ice in washtubs. Put gunny sacks over it."

"All right, son."

The boy left the hotel. Yates followed him toward the door and then seemed to feel that some explanation was in order. "I'm taking food and refreshments out to the posse. It's the least I can do for those boys."

"You taking any hard liquor?" Briley asked.

"Just beer. It's a good idea, though. I expect some of those yahoos would appreciate a snort."

"Don't," Briley said.

"Don't?"

Briley gave him a point-blank look. Yates nodded his acquiescence. "Denny, why don't you ride along

92

with me?"

"My business is in town," Wales said.

Yates hesitated another moment and then went into the street. Briley eyed Wales thoughtfully.

"Your business with the Gemini Ridge mine?"

"With the folks that own it—and a dozen like operations."

"Cyclops-Umatilla?"

"A step higher yet. North American Land & Livestock."

Briley's eyebrows went up. "Tackleman is on the hunt."

"He wouldn't talk to me, anyway," Wales said. "He'd pass me along to a flunky. I'll drop in on Mr. Gilly."

"Mr. Wales, what do you know about Tackleman?"

"You should know better than to ask a glary-eyed anarchist a question like that."

"I've read about you in the Butte paper," Briley said. "Hell, you're no anarchist."

"I'm a dreamer, Briley, a dreamer. And a socialist, but not your doctrinaire European socialist. I dream of an American socialism that will preserve a man's self-reliance and his dignity. A system as new and fresh—and as American—as the Constitution was in 1787. I didn't mean to make a speech, but you know us agitators."

"Tackleman?"

"A pirate."

"A killer," Briley said.

"All of them are killers at heart—all the financial muckamucks. They ruin their rivals with the greatest of relish. Tackleman is worse than most. His appetite for it overflows. He has to go out and kill literally."

Briley nodded grimly. "What else do you know about him?"

"Personally, very little. About his business operations, more than he'd like. But oh, no, Sheriff Briley, I'm not about to confide that particular information. It's my ace in the hole."

Briley stared absently into the sun-baked, almost lifeless street. He watched a thin young man in shabby range clothes tie his horse in front of the bank. The kid hesitated before the wide doorway for a moment; then, apparently mustering courage, he strode inside.

"Where did you know Yates?" Briley asked.

"Old Nowhere? First ran into him back in the old days in Butte when the railroad was building through."

"Nowhere. Kind of an interesting monicker."

"It's an interesting story if you haven't heard it."

"Can't say I have," Briley said.

"Well, once the NP got through Butte and over the Continental Divide, there were several different routes it could take. The favorite indoor sport was trying to guess which and get rich. There were two little mining towns in the plateau country there about ten miles apart—Annsdale and Bodie. It seemed a cinch that steel would be laid through one or the other, once the location engineers made up their minds.

"Yates came up with the idea of organizing his own railroad and laying track between the two towns. Whichever the NP went through, he'd have a spur to the other—a spur he figured he could sell to the NP at a big profit. It was more than just a wild idea when you take a hard look at it, and it was the kind of scheme high rollers were betting on in those days. So Yates got some backers who lent him the money he needed—at usurious interest, of course.

"The NP had had a touch of labor trouble—which explains the presence of yours truly—and the slowdown resulted in a backup of the supply system. There was steel piled along the tracks for miles. The story is, though he never admitted it, that Yates sugared off a superintendent or two and helped himself, hauling the rails at night in freight wagons. Anyhow, one way or another, he got what he needed and built his ten-mile railroad. Well, you guessed it. He no more than got his track down when the NP announced that it would run sixteen miles north of Annsdale—by-passing both towns.

"So Yates's railroad was a big joke. Folks started calling it the Nowhere and Lonesome. Pretty soon they were calling Yates 'Nowhere.'"

"And he ended up a horse trader," Briley said.

Wales gave him a puzzled look and went on talking. "But that's not the end of the story. Yates's backers were ready to lynch him—and there were those among them capable of it. But he didn't slope, I give him credit for that. He stayed around Butte, kind of a lost soul, making enough money gambling to pay the interest on his debt, I guess, and hoping to make a big killing—you know how gamblers are.

"What happened was that Amos Corner came along. He made the killing—and got Yates off the hook in the process."

"Whoa," Briley said. "Amos Corner?"

"The same. He had a medium important job with Umatilla Slate & Ore in those days."

"The same Amos Corner who's president of the bank across the street?"

"I'll be dipped," Wales said. "That's so. Amos inherited the bank from his uncle, old Si Corner."

Wales fished out his Bull Durham sack. Briley offered him a cigar, but he shook his head and dribbled tobacco into a brown cigarette paper.

"Well," Wales went on, "Amos had this scheme. He was close to Andy Laslow, who at that time was an ambitious young mining engineer. He talked Laslow into going in with him and taking an option on Yates's ten miles of track. Laslow then talked a group of investors into building a custom stamp mill at Bodie, provided the NP would build a spur to Annsdale.

"You see how it was. A spur to Annsdale meant a spur all the way to Bodie because of the Nowhere and Lonesome. A stamp mill meant that Umatilla's mines and a lot of others would send ore to Bodie to be processed. That meant business for the NP, and it agreed to build the spur. The next logical step was for it to buy the Nowhere and Lonesome, which it did. Yates got his debts paid. Corner and Laslow cleaned up."

"Tell me," Briley said. "How long has Yates been in the horse business?"

"The horse business? That's a new one on me."

"He drifted into my county last week with a string of trading horses."

"Well, it suits him, I guess," Wales said. "He's dabbled in one thing or another from time to time, but he's primarily a gambler. Picks up a living at the card table."

"Sort of a professional, would you say?"

"Sort of? He's a sure-thing professional—when he wants to be. Of course, the big-money players usually know who the sharps are. I imagine he has to travel around a bit and settle for smaller games."

"He's a sharp?"

Wales laughed. "He won't appreciate my mentioning it, but he's as slick a one-hand bottom dealer as you'll ever see."

Wales got to his feet and went to the desk, where he had a conference with the clerk and signed the register. Then he handed the clerk an envelope, which the clerk put into the hotel safe. As Wales turned toward the street door, Briley intercepted him.

"Are you *sure?*" Briley asked.

"At my age I'm not completely sure about anything," Wales said cheerfully. "But if you're speaking of Yates's digital dexterity, an agitator meets a lot of people, plays a lot of cards. He learns to spot a mechanic."

XI

Briley tarried in the shade of the hotel, watching Denny Wales quarter the street in a long, flat-footed stride and enter the building that housed the North American Land & Livestock office.

Wales, it had turned out, was well informed on the arcane technique of bottom dealing. He had pointed out that it was done chiefly with the third finger of the left hand and, once mastered, was as easy to do with one hand as two. Still, Briley didn't believe that Yates had cheated on that big hand Saturday night. True, he had dealt. But another player, Em Foster, had shuffled. Em could not possibly have been a confederate of Yates's. And what good would it do Yates to deal from the bottom if he didn't know what cards were there?

Briley crossed the street and went into the bank. The tellers' cages to the left of the entrance were constructed of heavy steel mesh. Their windows were barred, with a small space at the bottom where deposits and withdrawals could be pushed through. Whatever the practical value of this kind of fortification, typical of banks of the day, it gave customers the feeling that the management was in earnest about protecting their money.

Briley turned to the other side of the foyer, where there were two desks behind a low railing. One of the desks was occupied by a small, gray-haired man who looked up at Briley over low-riding spectacles.

"A man named Yates was in here about an hour ago," Briley said. "A one-armed man."

"Yes, sir, he was."

"Did he make a deposit?"

"Not that I know of." The man adjusted a desk plaque that said 'cashier.' "He met with Mr. Corner in Mr. Corner's office."

"I'd like to see Mr. Corner."

"He's busy at the moment, but he shouldn't be long. Come in. Have a chair."

Two minutes later a door at the back of the room opened and Amos Corner came out. He was with the thin young man Briley had seen through the hotel window. They were all smiles.

"I sure thank you," the young man said.

"Glad to be of help, Timbo," Corner said. "But I can't do the same for everybody, of course. So I'd just as soon word didn't get around."

"Absolutely not, Mr. Corner."

Briley entered Corner's office and sat down without waiting for an invitation. Corner sank into a swivel chair behind his desk and tilted back. The two knew each other only slightly, but neither seemed in a mood for formality.

"That lad," Briley said. "You called him Timbo."

99

"Timbo Dundee. A good boy with more spunk than luck, so far."

"What did he want?"

"Come on, Briley. I'm not going to discuss the kid's business affairs."

"The hell with his business affairs. Is he looking for his sister?"

"As a matter of fact, yes. He mentioned that he expected to find her at the North American office, but she wasn't there. He thinks she might be with the posse."

"She is."

"With Tackleman? . . . I supposed as much. I met her last night in his office."

Briley was interested. "How'd that happen?"

"I'd been trying to see him for several days about a business matter, but you know how great men are. No time for little country bankers. Last night when his car passed my house, I guessed he was headed for the North American office and I dropped in. He was on the phone. She was writing a letter."

"She's supposed to be working for him."

"And she's with him on a manhunt." Corner stroked his red necktie. "She's got no business there, Briley. She could get hurt."

Briley nodded somberly. "Mr. Corner, I'm told you're an old friend of Henry Yates."

"I've known him for years, but not very well. He was in here a little while ago."

"What did he want?"

"Just a friendly visit. Told me his troubles. That robber took most of his life savings. I hope you

100

recover it."

"You had business dealings with him some years ago."

"The Nowhere and Lonesome." Corner smiled faintly in reminiscence. "Those were wild days, Briley. We were young and venturesome."

"You made a lot of money on that deal?"

"I shared in a substantial profit, yes."

"And Yates didn't?"

Corner was a mild-mannered man, but for a moment he looked angry. "Look here. We got Yates out from under a crushing load of debt. He didn't expect to profit."

"Tell me, Mr. Corner. Is Yates a card shark?"

"He used to like his poker."

"I mean a sharper, a cheat."

"I—don't think so. A one-armed man?"

Briley left the bank wondering why Yates had said he made a deposit when he hadn't. It was a small lie perhaps, but why hadn't he said he had simply dropped in to chat with an old friend? The answer seemed to be that Corner, too, had been less than candid. They had discussed something important, and each in his own way had tried to conceal that fact.

Briley decided he would get his composition book from his saddlebags, go back to the hotel lobby, and write some of this down. Writing tended to clear his thinking.

As he turned toward the livery, a small commotion caught his attention. The town marshal was leading a man in handcuffs along the sidewalk toward the police station. Half a dozen men were following, protesting, trying to argue with the marshal. Briley stepped into the street for a better view. The man with his hands cuffed behind his back was Denny Wales.

Briley followed leisurely and at a distance. The police station was a small stone building in the middle of a block. The marshal hustled his prisoner up the steps and inside. When the protestors—miners, Briley guessed—tried to follow, a deputy appeared and posted himself in front of the door, keeping them on the steps.

Briley halted at the rear of the small crowd. "What did he do?" he asked one of the miners.

"Nothing. Not a frigging thing."

Briley called to the deputy. "What's the charge?"

The deputy shook his head, not knowing the answer or not deigning to give it. Briley moved up the steps. The deputy saw his badge and hesitantly stepped aside.

The marshal's office was a large room that took up the front of part of the building. The marshal, a tall man with a cropped mustache and a military bearing, was removing the handcuffs. He recognized Briley and nodded curtly. He asked about the manhunt, saying he had heard that Jackson was trapped and would probably be taken by sundown.

"Maybe," Briley said. "I just hope he's taken alive."

"Tomorrow is a better bet. It's my observation that fugitives generally wear themselves out by the third day."

An old theory, Briley thought. He said, "This one's a daddy coon."

Wales emptied his pockets and the marshal inventoried their contents. Twenty dollars and eleven cents, one blue bandanna, one Ingersoll watch, one toothbrush, one razor, one keyring with three keys, one pencil. . . . There were also matches and a sack of Bull Durham that he was allowed to take to his cell with him.

"What's he charged with?" Briley asked.

"He assaulted Mr. Gilly in the North American office."

"A lie," Wales said.

The marshal led him to a door at the back of the room with the jail keys hanging next to it on a big iron ring. One of the keys unlocked the door. The others were to the cells behind it. There were three cells—two small ones and a large one. The marshal locked Wales into the large one. There were no other prisoners.

Briley had followed them into the jail. The marshal gave him a questioning look when he lingered by Wales's cell.

"I'll talk to him," Briley said.

"You have an interest in this prisoner?"

"I might have."

The marshal eyed him sharply, then he gave a brisk, affirmative bob of his head and left them alone.

"I made a bad miscalculation," Wales said. "I thank you for coming."

"What'd you do—take a sock at Gilly?"

"Never laid a finger on him. Briley, I'm scared."

103

"Seems like you might have been in jail often enough to be used to it."

"Gilly's up to something. I can sense it. I never touched him, Briley, never even thought about it. What I'm guilty of might be called blackmail, but not assault."

"You tried to blackmail him?"

"In a sense, Briley, in a sense." Wales sighed mightily. "Labor has friends in strange places. That means I have spies in strange places. North American Land & Livestock has got control of Cyclops-Umatilla. That's hardly a secret any more. Tackleman did it. I learned how he did it and what his plans are. He's looting Cyclops, stripping it, pushing it into bankruptcy.

"I don't truly know how damaging that information is. Some of it will come out eventually, in any case. But I have evidence that he may be about to loot North American, too. For that to come out now would be, at the least, mighty embarrassing to him and his crowd.

"Well, Cyclops has shut down every mine it operates. That's part of the grand strategy, but an incidental benefit to management is going to be lower wages when the mines reopen. Base pay will be cut by a dollar a day or more—I know that for a fact. There's nothing the workers can do about it. Even if they were decently organized, which they aren't, a strike would be out of the question after a shutdown.

"So I went to Gilly and told him what I know about the plan to push Cyclops into bankruptcy and to strip it. He was shaken up, I could see that plain enough. I told him I'd keep my mouth shut provided I could have a promise, in the form of a public announcement by Tackleman himself, that wages will *not* be cut when the mines reopen. I told him if Tackleman refuses, I'll turn my information over to the *New York Times*."

"Well, he ordered me out of the office. I went down to the Silver Dollar, where I knew I'd run into some of the local miners. I wasn't there five minutes when the marshal walked in and put the cuffs on me."

"No witnesses to your meeting with Gilly?" Briley said.

"Just the two of us."

"That's good. He can't make an assault charge stick without witnesses." Briley added, "Not unless he's got some awful bad bruises."

"Damn it, Briley, the charge is one hundred per cent trumped up. He's got me locked up until he can decide how to shut me up."

"Calm down," Briley said. "He won't do anything until he talks to Tackleman. They'll probably drop the charges in the morning and let you go. Who knows? Your blackmail might even work."

"Not with that crowd—I can see that now. And Tackleman owns this town, you know that. He probably owns that broomstick marshal. I could die in here, Briley. It could be made to look like suicide. Or like I was killed trying to escape."

Briley nodded thoughtfully, looking around the empty jail. "I'll see if there's anything I can do."

"I made a mistake," Wales said. "These are big people. They destroy empires. They wouldn't think

105

twice about knocking off a raggedy-ass little labor spokesman who they consider an anarchist anyway."

Briley nodded again. It was true enough, he guessed.

"There's something else I want you to know," Wales said. "I wrote down everything I know about the Cyclops thing. It's in an envelope addressed to a reporter I know on the *New York Times*. Before I left the hotel, I gave it to the clerk to put in the hotel safe."

"This is your day to make mistakes," Briley said. "North American owns that hotel."

"God Almighty! Will you get it for me, Briley? I'll give you a note to the clerk."

"And what am I supposed to do with it?"

"Hold it, just hold it. Unless something happens to me. Then mail it."

"Can I read it?"

Wales was suddenly suspicious. "Why?"

"Why not?"

"You struck me as an honest man. Was that another mistake? You got some idea of putting the finger on Tackleman yourself?"

Briley regarded him steadily. "Mr. Wales, I've been a lawman a long time. If I leaned toward blackmail, I'd be either dead or rich."

Wales gripped the bars of his cell and sagged against them. "Sorry," he said. "But you can't read the damn thing. It's sealed." He grinned suddenly, revealing the gap in his teeth. "Go ahead and steam it open if you want to. Either I trust you or I don't. I guess I do."

Briley got the marshal, asked for pencil and paper,

and then had him witness Wales's signature on a note to the hotel clerk.

In the front part of the station, the deputy was inside now, standing at the door with his hand on the knob. The miners were still on the steps, Briley guessed.

"You keep a tidy jail," he said to the marshal.

"Try to."

"No other prisoners."

"I try to keep a tidy town," the marshal said.

"How do you feel about labor agitators?"

"Scum."

"I don't know," Briley said. "Sometimes I wish there was a union for us hick cops."

The marshal decided that was a joke and smiled stonily. The deputy opened the door for Briley, and he stepped out among the miners. He caught the arms of two of them and, walking between them, led them down the steps. The others clustered around as he halted on the sidewalk.

"Wales is scared," he said. "Maybe there's no reason for it, but he's alone in there. How far will you go for him?"

A moment later he was back inside the station with the two men in tow.

"I request the arrest of this pair," he told the marshal. "Disturbing the peace, obscene language, threatening behavior. I'll sign the complaint."

Surprise crossed the marshal's face, but he said nothing. He searched the prisoners, marched them off to jail.

"Company for you!" Briley called to Wales.

The marshal came back into the office, hanging up

the keys. "I'm glad to accommodate you, Sheriff. But just what in hell are you up to?"

"Seems like Wales ought to have the solace of a couple of sympathizers."

"Briley, are you suggesting something?"

"Nothing at all, Marshal. Wales is uneasy. I believe he'll feel better now."

XII

Jackson led his captors south and east toward the area where he had been that morning. He avoided his backtrail as much as possible, sometimes detouring circuitously. At one point, Schrockenmeyer jerked on the lariat that was looped around Jackson's neck and pulled him to a halt.

Jackson's temper flared. "You do that again and the deal is off. You'll coast through hell on a bobsled before you see that money."

"You're taking us roundabout every which way," Schrockenmeyer said.

"Of course I am! You want to run into other people from the posse?"

The chance of that was not great, Jackson guessed. A good many of the other possemen would have seen the smoke signal and would have headed for it. Those who had not—as his captors obviously had not—would probably have worked their way into the higher canyons by now. Still, there might be other stragglers like these three. So far, he had been able to stall them; but if they were joined by others, the game was over.

He had no plan except to stall and watch. These three were not experienced manhunters. If they had been, they would have found his sleeve gun, for one thing. Sooner or later they'll make another mistake, he told himself. A second or two of carelessness is all I need. Concentrate on the one called Perry. He has the shotgun. That will be the crucial factor—the shotgun.

"How much farther?" Perry asked petulantly.

"Hard to tell. A mile or so."

"You said two miles when we started out. You lost?"

"No."

"I sure am," Pinky Greene said.

Jackson waved them forward. Schrockenmeyer rode a few feet behind him, lariat end tied to saddle horn. In the narrow places Pinky and Perry fell back into file. After a few minutes they struck the route he had followed that morning. Half a dozen horses had been over it since.

They curled around the base of a hill, and Jackson glimpsed motion in a little rincon off to the right. He raised an arm to bring the others to a halt. The little pocket was cluttered with boulders with occasional twists of scraggly juniper among them. He pointed to a flashing form among the boulders.

The dog was there, leaping and scrambling around the rocks, chasing a marmot. The little animal dived into a burrow under a boulder. The dog began to dig frantically. Another marmot appeared on top of a big boulder to the right, emitting a soft, chattering whistle. The dog dashed after it, chain dragging.

"I'll be damned," Perry said. "He's got loose."

"Them rockchucks are playing with him," Pinky said. "They'll wear him down to a frazzle."

"You hear what Tackleman said this morning?" Perry said. "He said he wouldn't take a thousand dollars for that dog."

"Maybe he would now," Pinky said. "The critter has forgot all about manhunting."

"We could take him back," Perry said. "Tackleman ought to be pleased."

"What do we care if Tackleman is pleased?" Schrockenmeyer said. "Let's get moving."

"Wait up," Perry said. "We ought to catch that dog. We show up with it, that will sort of account for where we been and what we been doing. It will never enter anybody's head that we might have caught up with Jackson and got the money."

"You make no sense," Schrockenmeyer said.

"It's what you might call misdirection," Perry said.

"It makes sense," Pinky Greene said. "Only who's going to catch the brute?"

"You boys are crazy," Schrockenmeyer said. He gave a flip of the rope and motioned to Jackson to move on.

Jackson removed the noose from his neck. Schrockenmeyer drew his huge old Walker Colt, cocking it. Perry raised the shotgun.

"Take it easy," Jackson said. "I'll help you catch the dog."

"Put that rope back around your neck," Schrockenmeyer ordered.

Jackson disregarded him and looked over his

surroundings. This was the place and the time, he guessed. The rincon was roughly spade-shaped. It lay at the upper end of a ravine with nearly vertical slopes on both sides of it. There was no possibility of his making a run for it here; his captors would see no reason to keep him closely covered with their guns. The dog should provide plenty of diversion. This was where he would make his play.

He faced Schrockenmeyer. "The money is here."

"Here?" Schrockenmeyer said. "Whereabouts?"

"Buried in the rocks. The dog must have tracked me here."

"Go in and get it."

"Not much. Not till that dog is tied."

Perry and Pinky swung down from their horses and walked up to stand a few feet from Jackson. Perry held the shotgun at port arms. Pinky's revolver was in its holster. He kept touching its butt with his right fingers as if ready to draw it fast. He fancied himself in the role of a gunslick, Jackson thought, but he was probably far from expert.

"All right," Perry said to Jackson. "Go ahead. Tie him."

"Don't say we didn't warn you," Pinky said. "That dog is a trained mankiller."

"Right now he's a little mixed up," Perry said, "but he could get over it."

The dog was in a frenzy, trying to dig into a burrow. It was panting enormously, and its snout was covered with dirt. The burrow was in rocky ground between two adjacent boulders and impossible to enlarge very much.

"To rope him would be best," Schrockenmeyer

said. "Get two ropes on him."

Jackson waited, sensing that the others would object.

"He'd fight," Pinky said. "He'd pull himself to pieces."

"Wouldn't be easy to rope him among all them rocks, anyway," Perry said.

"Then I'll shoot the bastard," Schrockenmeyer said.

"And bring half the posse down on us?" Jackson said. "No, let's try to gentle him."

Pinky laughed. "That dog don't know gentle."

"We'll see," Jackson said. "Let me have my canteen."

Pinky went back to his horse and got it. Schrockenmeyer dismounted, still holding the big Colt. Jackson took the canteen and drank, fighting back a surge of weariness. He was soaked with sweat and beginning to feel a little wobbly from walking. He walked up to the dog, talking to it to make sure he didn't surprise it.

"Dig him out, boy! Dig, dig, dig! That's the boy...."

He took off his hat and pushed a bowl-like concavity into the crown. Still talking to the dog, he moved closer and set the hat on the ground. He picked up the dog's chain and worked up to a short hold on it close to the dog's collar.

"Come on, boy."

He pulled the big animal away from the burrow, raising it to its hind legs. It tried to turn on him, snapping and snarling, but he held it firmly at arm's length and spilled water from the canteen on the

113

dog's head. The dog writhed powerfully. Jackson spilled more water. The dog snapped at the water, getting a mouthful, swallowing it, getting another. Jackson swung the canteen toward his hat, moving the dog with it. He filled the depression in the crown with water and maneuvered the dog's head directly over it. The dog hesitated, then lapped greedily.

It did this only briefly, then it strained to get back to the burrow. A change had taken place. It was used to being controlled on a leash. However resentfully, it accepted a man's control now. It snarled and snapped the air in its eagerness to get back to the hunt, but it no longer tried to turn on Jackson. He pulled it farther away from the burrow, gave it more water. Grinning, he offered the chain to Perry.

"You want to hold him?"

"No, thanks," Perry said. "Tie the brute and show us the money."

Perry pointed to a twisted juniper growing from behind a boulder. Jackson backed the dog toward it. He handed the canteen to Schrockenmeyer. Then he told Perry to pick up the end of the six-foot chain.

"You tie it. I'll keep a short hold on him."

Perry moved back to the juniper and tied the chain, shotgun in the crook of his arm. Jackson and the dog were still facing the marmot burrow, the dog straining toward it. Jackson transferred his hold on the dog to his left hand, grasping the collar, palming the derringer from his left sleeve. His fingers worked at the buckle on the collar.

Schrockenmeyer and Pinky stood ten feet away and a little to the right. Schrockenmeyer holstered his gun, drank from the canteen, and passed it to Pinky.

Perry finished tying the chain and came up on Jackson's left, six feet away and with the dog between them. Jackson unbuckled the collar and loosed the dog.

It was easy enough then. In the second in which the dog, streaking toward the burrow, was the compulsive center of attention, Jackson leaped toward Perry with the derringer leveled at his head. Perry froze, let go of the shotgun as Jackson reached for it. Jackson stepped away and covered the others with it.

XIII

When they left camp that morning, Laura Jean had taken it upon herself to bring up the rear of the small party and to lead Jim Smoke's horse—since Jim walked ahead with the dog. But Mr. Tackleman wouldn't hear of that. He saw to it that one of the others led the horse and he insisted that Laura Jean ride beside him at the head of the party.

She enjoyed that sort of attention, she admitted. It made her feel important. But there was something about it that bothered her, too. I do just as he says, she thought. He's a distinguished financier and a handsome, dashing man, and he's my employer. I certainly want to please him. What's more, when he asks me to do something, he does it in a way that makes me *want* to do it. It's as if he thinks for me. I'll have to find a way to assert myself as a person, a perfectly reasonable way to say no to him. If I do it right, he'll have more respect for me.

Tackleman was in high spirits, concentrating on the hunt but talking and joking with everybody. He needled Jim Smoke pretty hard, especially after Jim lost the dog, but there was a good-natured note in his voice. Jim didn't seem to take it seriously and came back with needling of his own.

"You never liked the idea of working with Apache," Tackleman said when they had given up chasing the dog and Jim was back on horseback. "I think you let him go on purpose."

"I damn near let a couple of fingers go with him," Jim said.

"Maybe it wasn't such a bad idea to let him go. Maybe he'll catch up with Jackson and slow him down a bit."

"Not that dog," Jim said. "He don't know what he's after. He just wants to tear something to pieces, he don't care what."

Tackleman rode in thoughtful silence for a moment. Then he said, "I say he'll catch up with Jackson. You want to bet he won't?"

"How much you want to bet? A couple of million?"

"How about double wages or nothing?" Tackleman said.

"I'll tell you what. I've got a Crow scalp my grandfather took. It would look nice over your fireplace. I'll bet you that against fifty dollars."

"I've already got some scalps—a Comanche scalp pole."

"This is a black man's scalp. You got one of those?"

"I thought you said it was Crow."

"Crows adopted blacks into their tribe. In the old days some of their best warriors were blacks."

"I've read about them," Tackleman said, interested now. "Let's see—Jim Beckworth, York, a man named Rose. Has this scalp got kinky hair?"

"Not exactly."

"Then how do you know it's a black man's?"

"Grandpa said so."

"All right," Tackleman said. "It's a bet. If I lose, which I don't expect to, maybe I'll buy the scalp from you."

"Done." Jim's quick glance had a sly pleasure in it. The thought crossed Laura Jean's mind that he didn't have any such scalp at all.

When Jackson's trail became tangled or disappeared entirely, Jim got down from his horse and scouted while the other riders hung back. He always got them off in the right direction, but sometimes this took time. Sheriff Hornbill became impatient. Tackleman did not. He was a very controlled man, Laura Jean thought.

They saw the smoke signal then, and their pace picked up. They no longer worried about losing the trail and pushed their horses up the steep and tortuous route to the pass. Hornbill was elated now, yelling encouragement to the others and sometimes urging them to move faster than Jim Smoke and Tackleman considered prudent.

"Slow down," Jim Smoke finally said curtly. "And calm down. We're raising too much dust and making too much noise."

Hornbill glared at him and muttered a reply that Laura Jean didn't catch. For once he didn't yell.

They moved into sharp little ravines, traveling at a trot. Laura Jean decided she'd had enough and dropped back. Tackleman immediately joined her and asked what the trouble was.

"This mare trots like she's got three legs. I'll catch up later."

"Good Lord, girl." Tackleman had drawn the buffalo gun from its boot and was carrying it across his saddle. "We could run into our man any minute. It would be a shame to miss the kill."

"I'm sorry. I'm getting saddle sore."

"Come on," he said, flashing his bright grin. "Who isn't? Stick it out just a little longer."

They caught up with the others and resumed the lead. It happened again, she thought. I do everything he says.

They entered the valley at the summit of the pass, and a rider was there to meet them. It was the foreman from the Cipher Lake ranch. He galloped toward them with his right hand raised high as if afraid he would be mistaken for Jackson.

"He's got out of the valley," he reported as he reined up. "I wonder you didn't run into him."

Hornbill swore shamelessly. Except for a certain grimness, Tackleman showed no disappointment. He rose in his stirrups to scan the little valley, his eyes bright with this new challenge of the hunt. His look rested on the hills to the south.

"You sure he's not up there somewhere?"

"Yes, sir." The foreman gave an account of the encounter with Jackson.

"His horse was hit?" Tackleman said. "You're sure?"

"I had a clean broadside shot, and I dropped the animal. He got it into the draw, and it seems it carried him out of here."

"Where are your men?"

The foreman pointed to the canyon at the far end of the valley. "It seemed the best place. We could have let him come on and taken him, I guess, but you said to turn him back."

"Yes," Tackleman said. "I did."

The foreman looked at his watch. "He left the valley less than an hour ago. You must have missed him by a hair."

"Damn it, we should have spotted his back trail."

"We might have," Jim Smoke said with a glance at Hornbill, "but we came too fast."

They found it easily enough now and turned back with it. In spite of being on a wounded horse, Jackson had ridden in difficult and unlikely places in order to stay clear of his old trail.

"He's a cute one," Jim said. "Wouldn't surprise me if he's got some Indian in him."

"That's no recommendation," Tackleman said. "Here I am paying an expensive Indian tracker, and he let the quarry double back right under our noses."

"The what?" Jim said.

"The quarry. I thought you spoke English."

"Not millionaire English. Anyway, the dog didn't catch him. That's another fifty dollars you owe me."

"You lost that dog," Tackleman said. "I'm going to dock you for that."

He didn't mean it, of course; he was just needling. But Jim was piqued.

"That dog was an A-number-one bad idea from the beginning," Jim said.

Tackleman chuckled. "Just because you couldn't handle him?"

"A greenhorn millionaire idea."

Tackleman threw the Indian a sharp glance and didn't reply. It came to Laura Jean then that in spite of the mask of their lighthearted banter, these two weren't hitting it off. It had seemed at first that they might really have sort of a rough affection for each other. But they didn't.

Hornbill had become strangely silent except for a profane monosyllable or two. He cussed at his horse, at the heat, at every slight delay when Jim dismounted to study the trail. Sometimes after he had come out with a pelt-warmer, he glanced in Laura Jean's direction with a certain defiance.

They came to a creek and concluded that Jackson had turned down it, walking in the water and leading his horse. A few minutes later they came upon the horse, dozing in the shade of a big rock outcropping. Jim and Tackleman dismounted for a close look at the big buckskin. Tackleman raised his rifle and was going to shoot the animal, but Jim objected.

"Don't," he said. "No sense in it."

"The animal's hurt."

"He don't look that hurt to me, but that's not the point. Jackson's afoot now, so we're a lot closer to him than we were. A shot will tell him where we are."

"Not one shot." Tackleman cocked the rifle. "Not in these mountains."

"It will tell him exactly. He'll know we killed the horse."

Tackleman laughed, defeated by the simplicity of Jim's logic. He lowered the gun and eased down the hammer. "How did I ever get such a smart tracker?"

"Let's get moving!" Hornbill yelled, excited now that Jackson was afoot. "Did he go up the creek or down?"

"I don't know," Jim said.

They lost time while he scouted. He finally found the faintest remnant of a footprint upstream and well away from the creek. After a bit, the trace was clear enough, but it took them over steep, slow ground. They got into a narrow canyon and found Jackson had climbed a steep slope where horses couldn't follow. Jim pointed to a stand of pines at the top.

"He could be holed up there, waiting for dark."

"A real possibility," Tackleman agreed.

"I'll climb up on foot—and anybody else who wants to come along. The rest of you take the horses on down the canyon and see if there's a way you can get up there."

Tackleman was already dismounting. "Feel like a climb?" he asked Laura Jean.

"Not much. Not in this—" she was tempted to use one of Hornbill's adjectives—"dress."

"Come on." His hand was on her back, gently urging her from the saddle. "Our man may be up there in those trees. This may be the climax of the hunt."

"No, thanks," she said; but even then she was sliding from the saddle. He caught her and led her to the slope.

It seemed that she, Tackleman, and Jim were the only volunteers—if that was the word—for the climb. Tackleman was disturbed.

"Sheriff?"

"I'm too frigging old!" Hornbill yelled.

"I want another gun along."

One of the other men dismounted and joined them. "If our man's up there, I'm claiming a double share of the reward."

In places the climb was almost straight up. Laura Jean's dress was not only a handicap but sometimes a dangerous one. Tackleman stayed close to her and gave her a hand when she needed it. When at last they reached the top, they found the rest of the party there ahead of them. They had dismounted and were standing around waiting for Jim Smoke to read the tracks they had found.

"Looks like this manhunt is over!" Hornbill yelled. "Some of the boys has got him!"

Jim Smoke studied the sign and followed it a little way down a slope to the south. Laura Jean went to the edge of the trees and sat down with her back against one of them. Tackleman joined her. He sank down in a shady spot, took off his hunting cap, and wiped his face on his sleeve. He shrugged and grinned handsomely, but she sensed a deep and angry disappointment.

"It wasn't all for nothing," she said. "It's been exciting."

"He gave us a good chase," he agreed, "but apparently he didn't put up a fight. They've taken him alive."

"I'm glad."

She watched for his reaction, but he leaned back and closed his eyes as if he hadn't heard. For a moment he let his tiredness show, speaking almost drowsily. "He did give us a good chase."

Jim Smoke returned. He was frowning. "Three

riders," he said. "Jackson on foot, walking ahead. But they didn't head for camp. They turned south."

Hornbill gave him a blank stare. "What does that mean? They lost?"

"Don't see how they could be. Camp is straight east," Jim said, pointing. "You head straight down that canyon down there and you can't miss it."

"They drunk?"

"Could be," Jim said.

Tackleman got to his feet. "The money! He must have hidden it. They're making him take them to it."

Jim Smoke shook his head. "Maybe. Doesn't seem likely, though."

"Why not?" Hornbill yelled. "He run into some tough boys who used a little persuasion!"

"Maybe," Jim said again. "Only it doesn't seem to me that he'd cache the money—not till he found he couldn't get over the pass. In that case, he'd hide it somewhere along the trail we've been over."

Tackleman put on his hunting cap, giving a tug at its long bill. He headed for his horse. "Come on. This is worth looking into."

Laura Jean had been thinking about supper in the Cattlemen's Hotel dining room and taking a bath and crawling into a soft bed. But Tackleman's enthusiasm seemed to have returned, and that pleased her. She gave him a smile as he boosted her into the saddle.

In half an hour they reached the place where Jackson and his captors had halted. Jim dismounted, telling the others to stay back till he had a chance to look at the sign. He moved ahead, studying the ground. Then he straightened and pointed to the rocky little rincon. The dog was lying among the boulders, panting painfully.

The others saw it and dismounted. It was lying in front of a marmot burrow, watching it, too exhausted to dig any more. Jim pointed to its chain, tied to a juniper a few feet away.

"Looks like they tried to catch him for you," Jim said.

"Fool animal has been chasing varmints!" Hornbill yelled.

Laura Jean sat down on a boulder. Tackleman slowly approached the dog. It looked at him sideways and snarled. He backed off and went over and picked up the chain.

"They had him," he said. "He got away from them."

Jim Smoke laughed. "It takes a hell of a smart dog to unbuckle his own collar."

"Then what happened?"

Jim shrugged. He drifted a few yards down the ravine, studying the ground. He stood for a while with hands on hips, his back toward the others. He turned, slapping his sides, and came back smiling cynically.

"Three men walked out of here. Two of them were leading their horses. One man rode behind them."

Hornbill didn't hear and Jim had to say it again. Then he said to Tackleman, "I figure I still win my bet. Jackson caught up with the dog, not the dog with him."

Tackleman was staring at the dog as if trying to decide what to do about it. "I'd say that makes it a standoff."

125

"Not much. The dog was supposed to attack him. Instead, it helped him. He used that no-good snarling son of a bitch to get the deadwood on the others. I don't know how, but he did. Maybe I ought to claim you owe me double."

They mounted, Laura Jean again accepting a leg up from Tackleman. He lingered beside his horse as the others moved off on the new trail. The roar of his rifle was earsplitting in the close-walled ravine.

"You were right," he said as he caught up with Jim Smoke. "Apache was a no-good dog."

XIV

"Head shot," Tackleman said. "Right behind the ear. He never knew what hit him."

Jim Smoke said nothing, but Laura Jean could see that he disapproved. There was no good reason to kill the dog and she sort of disapproved, too, or she would have if she'd felt she had any right to. If anyone else had done it, it would have been just plain mean; but, she couldn't apply that word to Lloyd Tackleman.

He's different from ordinary people, she thought— not better, but different. He is a law unto himself. You don't have to like that, but you have to accept it. And he is too kind and considerate to be called mean.

Jim raised a hand, bringing the party to a halt.

"Listen," he said.

"You're the slowest damn tracker I ever saw!" Hornbill yelled. "What—"

"Shut up," Jim said.

They all heard it then, all except Hornbill—a distant, thinly echoing human voice.

"He-e-ey!"

"Ahead somewhere," Jim said. "Not far."

They rounded a hill, heard the call again, and followed it up a timbered slope. They found three men here, each sitting with a tree trunk in his embrace, hands and feet tied on the other side of it. They had heard Tackleman's shot and started yelling. Jim and the other men with the party quickly untied them.

Perry Rumbaugh and Pinky Greene were shamefaced and quiet. Schrockenmeyer was in a murderous rage.

"I'll see that devil again!" he vowed. "I'll find him and I'll kill him. I won't talk to the son of a bitch, I'll just kill him."

Perry began an explanation. "We had him cold, but he didn't have the money. We bore down on him a little bit, and he said he'd take us to it."

"He lied," Schrockenmeyer said. "Every word was a lie."

"Shut up," Perry said. "We came across the dog. Jackson said the money was where the dog was. It wasn't, but we believed him."

"If it was, it's still there," Pinky said. "He didn't take it with him."

"He caught the dog," Perry said. "Then he let him go. The bugger had a derringer we missed, and—"

"Never mind," Tackleman said. "We know about what happened. How far ahead is he?"

"An hour," Schrockenmeyer said. "Two hours, maybe."

"Not that long," Pinky said. "He said he figured we could work ourselves loose in an hour. Going by that—"

"How can you go by that?" Schrockenmeyer demanded. "You people got extra horses?"

"Sorry," Tackleman said.

"Then we can ride double?"

Tackleman turned away, not bothering to answer. "You gents have a long walk," Jim Smoke said.

Jackson's trail led back over ground they had covered earlier. The sun dropped behind the War Bonnet peaks. The air was quickly cooler, but they were all tired and nobody talked much. Tackleman showed less wear than the others, Laura Jean thought. He sat straight in the saddle, scanning the country ahead, his blue eyes alert. Jim Smoke rode in kind of a crouch, his eyes on the trail.

They reached the canyon behind the hogback where they had been early that morning. Here, Jackson had tangled his trail again. Their earlier tracks were here, and it was hard to make anything out. Jim Smoke finally decided that Jackson's three horses had gone off in three different directions.

One trail led up the canyon, another down, and the third over the hogback toward camp. It was the least likely, so the party split up and followed the other two. Laura Jean rode with Tackleman and Hornbill. They headed down the canyon, and after a short distance came upon a riderless horse grazing in a little side canyon. They turned back and rendezvoused with the other group, which had also picked up a riderless horse.

They followed the trail over the hogback then and found that Jackson had ridden just over the crest, turned west, and had gone up the canyon after all.

"He gambled a little time and he won," Jim Smoke said. "We lost another hour on him."

Tackleman laughed without much enthusiasm. "He surely makes a monkey out of my expensive Indian tracker." He looked thoughtfully at Laura Jean. She was tired and sore enough to cry, but she smiled to let him see she wasn't giving up.

"We're right where we were this morning," she said, "but so is he."

"He can't get south from here, not on horseback," Tackleman said. "He might double back down this canyon and find a way into the valley, but we'll set a guard down there. We've already got Cobweb canyon blocked. We've got the pass blocked. Jim, if you were in his shoes, what would you do?"

"Not much choice. Lie low and wait for a chance to slip past us."

"The question is when?"

"Anybody's guess."

"I'm asking for yours. Tonight?"

"Maybe. Maybe tomorrow. Maybe the Fourth of July."

"It'll be dark soon," Tackleman said. "I guess we're beaten for another day."

They were about the sweetest words she'd ever heard, Laura Jean thought.

The horses were sluggish, and it took half an hour to reach camp. When they were still a little distance away, they heard music, faintly and then louder as the breeze caught it—the zig-zag whine of a fiddle.

XV

Briley hesitated before the door of the North American Land & Livestock office. The upper part of the door was a frosted panel. It was far from soundproof and he could hear a voice from inside. A man was talking loud, almost shouting. He was on the telephone, Briley concluded, probably with a long-distance connection.

". . . Yes, but that's going to come out anyway. Lloyd's reconciled to it . . . I hope to talk with him this evening. The point I want to make now is that Wales doesn't matter. He can't prove anything without the help of his informer. It's the informer who matters . . . Yes, that makes sense . . . Good . . . Hogan? Of course I know him. Ralph Hogan . . . I agree . . ."

Briley opened the door and went into the office. Gilly bent over a desk with his lips close to the phone. He held the receiver in one hand and a cigarette in the other. He regarded Briley with raised eyebrows.

"Just a moment," he said into the telephone and then spoke to Briley. "I'm talking long distance. Do you mind waiting? In the hall, please."

Briley went back into the hall. He walked a few steps down the empty corridor and then minced back to the door.

". . . It has to be him then. It proves that paying a man double is no assurance you can trust him . . . As I remember, he'd had a quarrel with Laslow. That's how we got onto him . . . Find out what you can and stay near a phone tonight. I'll call you after I've talked to Lloyd. Say hello to Anna and the children for me . . ."

When Gilly opened the door, Briley was down the hall, lounging against the stair railing and chewing on a cigar. Gilly beckoned him into the office, and Briley introduced himself.

"I've heard of you," Gilly said, sliding behind his desk and sitting down. He waved Briley toward a chair, but Briley stayed on his feet. "Didn't we make a contribution to your last campaign?"

"We?"

"North American."

"Fifty dollars," Briley said. "You also contributed fifty dollars to my opponent."

Gilly smiled and made a throwaway gesture. "We like to make sure."

"I'm here about Denny Wales, Mr. Gilly. You've charged him with assault."

"Not formally. Not yet. What's your interest in him?"

"He didn't assault you, Mr. Gilly. He threatened to expose certain information embarrassing to Mr. Tackleman."

"What's your interest in this, Mr. Briley?"

"He's scared," Briley said. "He thinks you might

132

have him assassinated."

Gilly sighed and produced an exasperated look. "The man must be a little insane. He was arrogant and abusive. I thought I'd teach him a little lesson. I had him jailed."

"Mr. Gilly, I ask that you either press charges or have him released."

Gilly exhaled through puffed cheeks. He stared thoughtfully at the telephone. Then, to Briley's surprise, he nodded agreeably.

"The fact is that subsequent developments—well, I've cooled off a bit. But you haven't answered my question. What is your interest in Denny Wales?"

"He might be helpful to me in a matter I'm looking into."

"May I ask what?"

"I'm looking into the background of a man Wales knows."

Gilly nodded again, apparently satisfied. "Shall we go down to the station?"

It seemed too easy, and Briley was suspicious. But Gilly accompanied him to the station. A few minutes later Wales was free. Briley dropped charges against the two miners, and they were released, too.

Gilly lingered behind, obviously wanting to talk with the marshal. Briley and Wales started down the street toward the hotel. Wales was far from being elated by his release.

"I know why Gilly had me jailed now," he said. "He has that marshal in his pocket and the deputy, too. He instructed them to get the name of my spy in the Cyclops organization out of me."

"Cheer up," Briley said. "I'd say they didn't get it."

"That's what bothers me. They took me out of my cell, handcuffed me, and took me to a bare little room at the back of the station. They made me sit down on the floor, and they questioned me. They kept coming back to the same question: 'Who is your informant at Cyclops?' They didn't get really rough, but they had a rattlesnake in a box back there. Afer a while they said they'd be back and talk to me later. They took off my shoes and cuffed my ankles together and left me alone there with that damn snake. It wasn't a very big box and I was scared to death the snake would get out. Then they came and got me and you and Gilly were there and it was all over."

They reached the hotel and sank into chairs by the window again. Wales got out his Bull Durham and began to spin up a cigarette. His fingers were trembling.

"There's only one reason Gilly dropped charges against me," Wales said. "He got the information somewhere else. Or he figured it out."

"He got it by telephone," Briley said.

"He told you that?"

"I overheard him on the phone."

"You read that letter I gave you?"

"Not yet."

"Well, the name is in there."

"Hogan," Briley said, "is a name Gilly mentioned."

"Stupid!" Wales said. "I was stupid! I wanted to scare Gilly with what I knew and I told him too much. They guessed that my information had to come from Hogan. They'll nail the poor devil to a door."

Wales licked the seam of his cigarette and held a

134

shaky match to it. "Stupid!" he said again. "You see, Hogan's an insider. Not a big-gun insider but a Cyclops accountant that they gave a big raise in pay and took into their confidence. They didn't know his brother was crippled by a strikebreaker at North American's Daylight mine four years ago. Hogan's had a grudge against Tackleman ever since. He confided the whole story to me, good old Denny Wales, whom he thought he could trust. He said that when the time was right, he was going to release the whole story to the press, along with enough incriminating evidence to paper a wall. But good old Denny Wales had to jump the gun!"

Briley had been staring absently at the street. It had been almost empty this morning, but now there was a good bit of traffic. Spring wagons, buggies, buckboards, even a couple of surreys had rattled past. There were riders, too, cowhands and youngsters. It was the kind of traffic you would expect on a Saturday afternoon, not on a Monday.

"I underestimated Gilly," Wales said. "I overplayed my cards. I told him enough so he could get on the phone to somebody in Butte and they could figure out my information had come from Hogan. Handle him, and you handle the whole problem. Without him and his evidence to back me, I'm just a wild-eyed radical making charges nobody would believe. And God, Briley! I betrayed the man."

In addition to the amount of it, there was another remarkable thing about the traffic. Not much of it was stopping in town and it was all headed in one direction. West. Toward the War Bonnets.

"I'll be off to Butte on tomorrow's stage," Wales

said. "I suppose I'm safe enough here for the night—I'm not important enough for Tackleman's bunch to bother about—a blow to my vanity. Still, I won't sleep too easy in a hotel owned by North American."

"Can you ride a horse?"

"Provided it's a sensible horse."

"I'm going back to camp. Why don't you come along?"

"Into the lion's den?" Wales said. "Why not?"

They bought food at the general store and at the bakery, and they packed it into flour sacks. They rented a horse for Wales at the livery stable and set out, galloping past a spring wagon to get out of its dust. A little later a buggy overtook them, drawn by a gaited bay traveling at a swift and showy four-beat rack. Gilly was driving it. He passed them with a curt nod.

"What do you think they'll do about Hogan?" Briley said.

Wales shook his head. "I imagine that's what Gilly is going to ask Tackleman."

XVI

Laura Jean and the others reached the camp in early twilight and were stunned by the change that had come over it. Her companions dismounted and began to unsaddle, but she continued to gawk, not sure whether she was going to be excited or distressed.

Half the town and most of the countryside was here, she guessed, and it was like a Fourth of July picnic. Families sat around tablecloths spread on the ground and were eating out of picnic baskets. People were lined up at the window of a sip-and-bite wagon, buying ice cream cones. In the back of a platform wagon a fiddler in a red-striped shirt and blue sleeve garters, a bearded man with a mouth organ, and a pimply kid with a Jew's harp stomped out "Old Dan Tucker." Nobody was dancing yet, but girls were clustering, hoping to be asked. Most of the possemen had returned and were gathered around a wagon where a one-armed man was passing out beer, biscuits, and fried chicken.

Tackleman came over and gave Laura Jean a hand down from the saddle. He regarded the scene sternly and then smiled tightly as he turned to Hornbill.

"This is something to be kept under control."

"Yes, siree!" Hornbill had a gleam in his eye.

The one-armed man waved at them from the back of his wagon. "Food and beer for the posse! Free gratis, compliments of Henry Yates!" Hornbill strode off in his direction. Tackleman went off to talk to Hurley, who was sitting in the Mercedes.

Laura Jean uncinched her saddle and was pulling it off Flag's back when somebody came up from behind and gave her a hand with it.

"Timbo!"

"Hi, Laura Jean." He set down the saddle and laid a hand on Flag's sweaty neck. "Guess you've been working her pretty hard."

"Yes, I have."

He looked the mare over carefully, apparently more interested in her than in his sister. It was what you expected of Timbo, and she didn't feel slighted. He was really pretty concerned about her, she guessed, or he wouldn't have come all the way from Langtown.

"You here on business?" she asked.

"I got your note. A man from the livery brought it out in the middle of the night like it was a telegram or something. I wanted to see Mr. Corner at the Table City bank about a loan anyway, so I came on down. What's this job you got? Deputy sheriff?"

"Don't be sarcastic." She pointed toward the sip-and-bite wagon. "Let's get an ice cream cone."

"I already had one."

He busied himself rubbing down Flag with the saddle blanket. She watched, thinking that it was nice to see him, even if he did have just terrible manners.

"How's Sally?" she asked.

"Fine. Baby's due the end of next month."

"I'm sorry I won't be able to be there to help now, but Timbo! I have this really good job with North American Land & Livestock and I'm going to live at the hotel and—"

"At the *hotel?*"

"What's wrong with that?"

"I didn't say there was anything wrong with it."

"Well, you gave me a funny look."

He gave her another and didn't reply. He finished rubbing down the mare and led her to the water wagon. There were twenty-gallon milk cans on the ground near the wagon, and he tipped water out of one of them into a bucket. Laura Jean went over to the sip-and-bite wagon. She had to wait in line and by the time she finally got a vanilla ice cream cone, Timbo had turned Flag into a rope corral with the other posse horses.

He went over and stood in a group that ringed the Mercedes, and she joined them. Hurley was sitting protectively in the driver's seat, curtly answering questions and swiping at kids who tried to climb aboard.

"You rode in it?" Timbo asked.

"I drove it."

"Laura *Jean.*"

"I did." Smiling at Hurley, she beckoned to Timbo and climbed into the back seat. He went around to the other side and climbed in beside her.

"How fast will it go?" He aimed the question at the

back of Hurley's head, but Laura Jean answered.

"This is the most powerful auto-mo-bile built. It has four cylinders and thirty-five horse power. It will go fifty miles an hour on a paved road."

"Your ice cream cone is dripping," Timbo said.

He got out of the car and led her to a place near the horse corral. They sat down on a little slope and watched a man pitch hay to the horses from the back of a wagon while she finished the ice cream cone. Finally, Timbo broke the silence.

"What about this job you got?"

"I told you. I work for North American."

"What kind of work?"

"Office work. I haven't started yet."

"What are you doing riding around with a posse?"

"It just happened." She told him about meeting Jackson and trading Flag and buying her back and driving the Mercedes and staying at the lodge and taking a bath and following Jackson's trail every which way and how sore her backside was.

"The job will probably only last until September," she said. "But Timbo! I make fifteen dollars a week and if I can get a job in Missoula for my room and board, I can start college. This fall."

Timbo looked around the camp until he located Tackleman and scowled in his direction. "How do you know he just wants you to work for him? How do you know he doesn't want something else?"

"He does not!" she said—too quickly. "I met Mrs. Tackleman and she's very nice and there's no reason why I shouldn't take the job."

"Fifteen dollars a week is too much."

"Not if you can get it."

He threw his Sunday punch then. "Mother wouldn't approve."

Laura Jean didn't answer because she was afraid she would either cry or lose her temper.

"I guess that wasn't fair," Timbo said.

Jim Smoke, who was a neighbor of Timbo's, joined them then. He was loaded down with three paper plates of fried chicken. "With the compliments of the victim of the crime," he said. He sat down with them and talked with Timbo about ranching, and they ate the fried chicken. Hornbill came over, a bottle of beer in his hand, and yelled at them that the posse was gathering for instructions and that Jim ought to be there. Jim traipsed off toward the meeting place, and Laura Jean and Timbo decided to follow.

The meeting place was only about a hundred yards up the canyon, but Tackleman and Hornbill arrived in the car, sitting in the back seat with Hurley driving. Tackleman stood up and addressed the posse.

"Now that Jackson knows he can't get over the pass, it's possible he'll try to slip out of the mountains on this side. We have this canyon blocked, of course, but there's another canyon about two miles south, a very small one, that Jim Smoke thinks might give Jackson a possible way out. He was there this afternoon but turned west again deeper into the mountains. We have to deal with the possibility that he'll double back again and try to get out that way. So Sheriff Hornbill will set up a guard there."

A groan surged through the tired posse. Tackleman grinned and went on, pointing upcanyon to a place where towering rimrock bellied out the canyon wall on both sides. The space between was only about fifty yards.

"We want another guard there, just in case. In both places we'll space out half a dozen lanterns so the area is well lighted. . . ."

"The bastard!" Jim Smoke said.

"Who?" Timbo said.

"If Jackson has any idea of sneaking out, he'll see the lanterns and know he's blocked," Jim said. "The guards will have no chance to take him. Tackleman wants to keep him bottled up so he can track him down."

"How would *you* do it?" Laura Jean demanded, sounding snappy and getting a critical look from Timbo.

"The guards ought to wait in the dark," Jim said. "Jackson could blunder right into them." He shook his head and added, "The great hunter wants a shot at the man with his Sharps. He was hoping for it all day."

Laura Jean set her jaw hard. She was angry and she was frightened. She didn't understand what had happened to her. She didn't approve of things that Lloyd Tackleman had done, yet Jim's disapproval of the man infuriated her.

"He's a law unto himself," she said.

Jim didn't reply and they listened to Tackleman's instruction to the posse. Three guards at the canyon mouth to the south. Two at the narrow place in this canyon. Two-hour watches. Four horses to be kept saddled all night. . . .

The meeting ended with Hornbill naming men for the first watch. The posse drifted back toward the camp. The Mercedes stopped on its way back, and Tackleman got out. He came over to walk beside Laura Jean, and she introduced him to Timbo.

"We'll stay in camp tonight," he said to Laura Jean. "Just to be sure we don't miss anything. Probably the most comfortable place to sleep will be in the car." He added, "You, too, Timbo, if you're staying."

Dusk was thickening here at the base of the mountains, although sunlight still touched the crest of the ridge across the valley. It was cool, too, and fires blazed in the camp. The music was going strong. Four couples had formed a square and were dancing. Others were prancing around every which way. A shadow moved toward them out of the firelight, calling to Tackleman. It turned out to be Mr. Gilly, and they went off together for a private talk. Jim Smoke headed for Yates's wagon and a beer.

"Does Sally expect you back tonight?" Laura Jean asked her brother.

"I told her to expect me when she sees me." He managed to sound independent to the point of callousness, but he was really a very devoted husband. He brightened and said, "Besides, I solved our financial problems. She'll be so happy about that—"

"You solved them?" Laura Jean said doubtfully.

"With the help of Mr. Amos Corner."

"That's—wonderful. Did he lend you more money?"

"Well, in a way," Timbo said. "I promised him I

143

wouldn't spread it around, but I guess I can tell you. You mustn't say a word to anybody."

"All right."

"The Table City bank already holds a second mortgage on my land, and Mr. Corner said he couldn't lend me another penny on it. But he's a very decent man, for a banker. He showed me a way to make some quick money and get out of the bind I'm in. It's kind of complicated; I don't know if you can understand it."

"I'll try."

"Well, he told me about this mining stock. Cyclops-Umatilla. All the mines are shut down and the stock has dropped from twenty-five down to four and a half."

"I know. I heard Mr. Tackleman and Mr. Gilly talking about it."

"Mr. Corner loaned me a thousand dollars, and I bought two hundred shares from the bank at five. In other words, the bank made a profit of half a point. He said he had to do that to make the deal look good on the bank's books."

"You bought two hundred shares? Oh, Timbo."

"Wait. He's holding the stock as collateral for the loan. See? I can't lose. He says the stock will go up to fifteen, maybe twenty, within a month—as soon as the mines open. That means I'll make enough to pay back the loan and have a profit of two or three thousand dollars!"

"Oh, Timbo!"

"He's not like your ordinary banker. He'll do a person a favor."

"Timbo, that stock is no good."

"Laura Jean, Mr. Corner says—. What do you know about stock?"

"I told you. I heard Mr. Tackleman and Mr. Gilly talking. Mr. Corner doesn't know what he's doing. Cyclops-Umatilla is going to go broke!"

"Boy-oh-boy! You sure became a financial expert in a hurry."

"I'm sorry. I guess Mr. Corner really is trying to do you a favor. You said he took the stock for collateral. I guess that's just another deal he's going to lose on. I can't talk about it because it would be betraying a confidence of my employer."

"Tackleman can be wrong just as easy as anybody else," Timbo said desperately.

"I don't think so. Not about a thing like this."

XVII

The man called Jackson lay against the canyon face on a ledge twenty feet above the ground. He had been there a long time, dozing a bit and watching the lanterns and the shadows that moved among them.

He could see the fires and hear the music beyond the lanterns at the canyon mouth. If the hoedown was big enough and wild enough, he could perhaps walk right through it without being noticed, he thought. But he could see no way to get past the lanterns. He had determined that there were only two guards and that the watch was changed every two hours, but that helped him not at all.

He was bone tired, and it was difficult to stay awake. If he'd got over the pass this morning, it would be over and he'd be clear by now, he thought. He'd have had a bath and a meal and be asleep between clean sheets. 'To sleep, perchance to dream?' Was that the rub? He could deal with the dreams, he thought.

He'd left his horse in a little side canyon a quarter mile back. It would be found in the morning, he guessed. Or would it? He worried about the horse. And the other, the wounded one. And the two he had killed at the pass. He hoped there wouldn't be horse-killing in his dreams. He didn't like to kill animals. He remembered his first deer. He was nine years old, and it was a quick, clean shot. His grandfather had been proud. "No buck fever for you," he said. But when they reached the deer, the tears had come in a torrent that he couldn't control. "That's good," Grandfather had said. "Remember that you cried and that it's an honorable thing."

A sound from up the canyon stabbed him to alertness. Someone was up there and coming this way. More than one person. They were afoot and they were grumbling and swearing. One of them saw the lanterns.

"What in the merry hell?"

Jackson recognized the voice as that of the cowboy called Perry. The others had to be Pinky and Schrockenmeyer.

"They got a guard there."

"Whoa up. We could get our tails shot off."

They came to a stop almost directly below Jackson.

"Yell," Pinky said. "Let 'em know we're coming. Hello-o-o!"

They moved forward, spreading out a little, all three hooting and hollering. A silhouette appeared among the lanterns, then another. Jackson eased himself off the ledge and began to climb down.

"Shut up!" Perry said. "Give 'em a chance to answer."

"Who-o-o's there?"

147

"We are, damn it! Don't shoot!"

"How many?"

"Three!"

"Come ahead slow! Come into the light!"

Jackson reached the canyon floor and slipped quietly along the south wall. This wouldn't do, he decided. The men were not walking down the middle of the canyon but were close to this side. He sat down, pulled off his boots. Clutching them, he started boldly across the canyon behind the three men.

It was safe enough as long as he made no noise. The three in front of him weren't likely to look back. The guards wouldn't be able to see anything beyond the reach of the lanterns. He ran easily in his stocking feet, boots in one hand, Winchester in the other. He reached the north wall and moved around bulging rimrock toward the lantern-lighted gap. He waited while the three men moved into the light near the south side of the gap. They were joined by the two guards and halted in a dark knot among the lanterns.

A lantern stood a yard from the wall on Jackson's side. He put his back to the wall and slid through the splash of light. Then he was quickly around the projecting rock and into the darkness of the widening canyon.

He pulled on his boots and watched the three men leave the guards and trudge into camp, silhouetted against the bonfires. Staying in the thick shadow of the wall, he moved closer to the camp. The music was loud and fast, and dancers were cavorting in the firelight. The party had turned pretty wild, it seemed, which was so much the better.

He studied the camp, picking out the car, the horse corral, and in the semidarkness on the far side, four saddled horses standing at a makeshift hitchrail. Reassured by the camp's absorption in itself, he stole still closer.

XVIII

Timbo strolled off toward Yates's wagon, saying he guessed he'd have a beer. Laura Jean could see that he was upset by what she'd said about Cyclops stock, even though he took the attitude that she didn't know what she was talking about. Mr. Corner was an old fool, she thought, albeit a generous one. He undoubtedly was trying to do Timbo a favor but was just building him up for a devastating disappointment.

Gee whiz, she thought. North American is going to take over Mr. Corner's bank. Is it going to take over the ranches of every hard-pressed little cattleman who has a loan there, too? Is it going to own the whole world?

Tackleman and Gilly were standing beside Gilly's buggy. She watched Tackleman take off his hunting cap and smooth back his wavy hair. She thought how good-looking he was and how powerful. Indians believed in power as a quality that a person acquires supernaturally. It seemed to her that there was some truth in that. Tackleman's power was part of the man, a personal quality. All his money and his influence were just a reflection of it.

It was the kind of power a medicine man has, she thought—or the devil. The idea was disturbing. I'm under his spell, she thought. I'm not Laura Jean Dundee but whomever and whatever he wants me to be. It's partly because he will pay me fifteen dollars a week and I want to go to college. Mostly it's because he is who he is.

It looked as if Gilly was about to leave, and she walked over to them, hanging back a little as she drew near.

"Don't wait for tomorrow's stage," Tackleman said. "Leave for Butte right away. Drive all night. Change horses at North American ranches along the way. You ought to be there fairly early in the day."

"I'm still not clear on—what you think should be done."

As he had been last night, Gilly seemed reluctant to talk in front of Laura Jean, but Tackleman smiled at her and beckoned her closer. He could make you feel trusted and welcome, she thought. It was part of his charm, part of his power.

"I want you to *handle* it," he said to Gilly. "Find out exactly what Hogan can testify to and what embarrassing documents he has access to. Then clear it up. Everything. The documents and the man."

"Without the documents, he'll be pretty impotent, won't he? Maybe if we throw a first class scare into him, that will be enough."

"It's up to your judgment," Tackleman said. "But I don't want any maybes. Learn the details, including the man's weaknesses. Then do what you have to. Gad! It's a wonder the man hasn't gone to Laslow."

"They had a quarrel. Laslow was going to fire him. That's how we got him into our camp in the first place."

"It could still happen. You haven't any time to lose."

Gilly nodded, his lips tight. He climbed into the buggy and they watched him drive away. Tackleman's hand pressed the small of Laura Jean's back and turned her toward the fires.

In spite of the fact that a banjo player had shown up and the music was livelier than ever, some of the families had gone home, disappointed in the hope of seeing Jackson brought in, but, likely as not, planning to come back tomorrow. There were few women left, and only two couples were dancing. Laura Jean and Tackleman were walking in time to the music; for a moment she was sure he would press her into his arms and dance with her. But a series of whoops brought them to a stop. They turned to see old one-armed Yates running to greet a wagon that was pulling up, loaded with women.

The wagon had bench seats rigged in the bed, and there were ten women in it, not counting the bulging, overdressed madam who rode with the driver. Yates's whoops were taken up by others. Half a dozen possemen converged on the wagon to help the girls down. The musicians swung into "There'll Be a Hot Time in the Old Town Tonight." Men swept up squealing partners, and dancing began in earnest. Somebody stirred up the fires, and the party exploded in the night.

Tackleman watched sternly. "Where's Hornbill?"

he muttered.

Actually, Hornbill was among the dancers, cake-walking with the bulging madam and waving a whiskey bottle with his free hand. It was a moment before Tackleman saw him. Then he strode forward and pulled him to one side. Hornbill grinned and offered the bottle, which Tackleman regarded disdainfully.

"Isn't it time to put the brakes on, Sheriff? We've got a guard to maintain."

"I'm changing it every two hours!" Hornbill yelled. He was more than a little glassy-eyed.

"Who brought hard liquor into camp?"

"The victim of the crime is desirous of showing his appreciation to the posse comitatus! He had a case of Old Crow under the wagon seat!"

"It seems to me you ought to confiscate it," Tackleman said. "We can't have drunken men going on guard."

Hornbill apparently didn't hear clearly. He grinned, swaying with the music. "These boys been in the saddle two solid days! Do 'em good to work the kinks out!"

Tackleman turned on his heel and strode toward a small fire on the edge of the camp. Laura Jean followed. Timbo, Jim Smoke, Sheriff Briley, and another man were sitting around the fire. Briley had rigged a lantern on a stick and was writing in his composition book. The others had bottles of beer and were passing around a bottle of whiskey. Ordinarily Timbo was no drinker, and Laura Jean was surprised to see him accept the bottle and take a pull at it.

153

The fourth man in the group grinned across the fire, displaying a gap in his front teeth. Tackleman nodded at him.

"Mr. Wales, I believe."

"Mr. Tackleman."

"I heard you were here." Tackleman spoke the words crisply, getting a special meaning into them. Then he said pleasantly, "You're a little out of your territory, aren't you?"

"Ah, Mr. Tackleman, your territory *is* my territory."

Tackleman turned to Briley. "Hornbill's drunk."

"It's his county," Briley said.

"He has no deputy here," Tackleman said. "Somebody ought to take the reins—confiscate the whiskey and send those women away."

"True enough."

"You could do it. I'd back you up."

"If I was in charge, Mr. Tackleman, the first thing I'd do, I'd send you home."

"My God, man. If I hadn't sent my men to block the pass, your fugitive would be long gone by now."

"In my opinion," Briley said, "that might have been the best thing that could happen."

"My God, are you drunk, too?"

"I've been toying with the idea all day. So far, I've only had a bottle of beer."

Tackleman turned away, patently disgusted. They walked back toward the dancing.

"People!" he said. "Without strong leaders, they are just a race of apes." He touched her elbow. "Let's take a drive down the valley. Just the two of us."

"What for?"

154

"I want to check on the guard down there."

"How long will we be gone?" She was surprised at her own coyness. The thought of driving off into the darkness alone with a millionaire in a Mercedes automobile was exciting, flattering, terrifying. I do everything he asks, she thought. Or I don't. Why don't I just say yes or no?

Timbo grabbed her by the other elbow and sashayed her into the melee of dancers. It was scandalous, she supposed, to be dancing among all these loose women, but just about everything she'd done in the last two days had been scandalous. Timbo was maybe a little drunk, but he was a good dancer. She felt the music, let it take hold of her, and found herself laughing out loud.

Tackleman watched for a moment. Then he went over to the car, and she lost sight of him. He didn't drive off down the valley to check the guards, though, and she wondered if he would ask her to go with him later.

She had another dance with Timbo and then found herself paired with the gap-tooth man called Wales. He was feeling his whiskey and did a lot of whooping and cavorting. Then melon-shaped old Em Foster puffed through a dance with her. Pinky Greene, who had just got into camp, was next, but he was footsore and gave up. He took her to the sip-and-bite wagon for another ice cream cone.

They stood in the twilight reach of the fires, sucked ice cream, and watched. Wales was dancing with first one girl and then another, bouncing and caracoling by himself in between. Timbo was dancing with a peroxided nymph, who in some of her more limber moments displayed a pair of pink garters. Laura Jean thought of Sally and the baby-on-the-way and wondered if her brother was too young to measure up to all the responsibility he'd taken on. Now and then a man would dance his partner out of the firelight and they would disappear into the darkness. If Timbo did that, she would go after him and bring him back, she decided—by the ear if necessary.

Denny Wales was putting into practice a theory he had long advocated. When you've had a bit too much of the wet goods, exercise. Pitch hay, hoe a garden, run a mile, swing Indian clubs. Or in this case, dance. It will sober you up in no time, and you'll not have a head in the morning. If folks were saying, "Look at the drunken anarchist," it wouldn't be the first time.

Before long he was sweating like a racehorse, and he slowed down a bit. Then he strolled away from the fires and up the canyon a way, savoring the cool darkness. A figure moved out from the canyon wall to intercept him, a tall man carrying a rifle.

"I've been watching you, Denny, hoping you'd wander this way."

Wales moved closer, squinting into the dark bearded face to make sure the night and the booze were not playing him tricks.

"Mother of God!"

"I know I can trust you, Denny. I also know it's going to cost me."

"You!"

156

"Listen to me, Denny."

"You—you're Jackson?"

"I need your help."

"You got this far. You can just walk out. There are saddled horses on the far side of camp."

"That won't quite do. How about a dollar a day, Denny?"

Wales took a deep breath and tried to gather his wits. "But you—"

"Take a chance, Denny. I think I can deliver."

"Mother of God! Yes, whatever it is you want, it's going to cost you a dollar a day."

Pinky finished his ice cream cone. Laura Jean was down to the last two inches of hers. She bit off the tip and sucked the ice cream through the bottom. For a boy who had a reputation as a girl-chaser, Pinky was strangely reserved. Yesterday he had been brash; tonight he seemed a little in awe of her.

The musicians were playing "Oh, Susanna." The dancers milled in misty dust, rose-tinged by the firelight. They, the camp, and the world seemed unreal. Denny Wales came high-stepping out of the darkness on the other side of the fires, bumping a man who stood drinking from a bottle. The man was Schrockenmeyer. He was in his stocking feet and held the bottle in one hand and his boots in the other. He spilled whiskey all over himself, and he barked angrily at Wales.

Wales danced away a few feet, moving backward. Then he danced up and punched Schrockenmeyer on the nose.

Schrockenmeyer staggered, dropping boots and bottle. He roared and drove forward, head down, arms spread, catching Wales around the waist. Their momentum carried them among the dancers. There they went down, kicking, punching, rolling.

The dancers splashed into a circle, cheering and squealing. Men dashed across the camp for a closer view, Pinky among them.

Someone grabbed Laura Jean from behind, his arm around her waist, his other hand over her mouth. There was something hard pressing against her stomach.

"That's a derringer," Jackson said. "A pistol. It's cocked."

She looked down and saw that it was indeed a gun. The crowd around the fighters was whooping and screaming. The musicians struck up "The Star Spangled Banner." Jackson took his hand away from her mouth.

"It isn't likely that anybody will hear you if you scream, but if you do, I'll shoot you."

He stooped to pick up a rifle he had laid on the ground, still embracing her tightly. He swept her across the edge of camp toward the horses that stood saddled and ready at the southeast corner. They were well out of the light except for that of Briley's lantern, rigged on a stick. They passed within a few yards of that, and Briley was still beside it, still writing in his book. Even if he had looked up, the light would have been in his eyes. He would have seen only the shadowy figures of a man and a woman hurrying off somewhere.

They reached the horses. Jackson ordered her to untie reins. Still holding her tightly, he marched her fifty yards down the valley before they mounted. They headed south, the reins of her horse in his hands. She spoke for the first time.

"What do you want with me?"

"You're a hostage," he said.

XIX

Laura Jean wondered how soon she would be missed and if her absence would be connected with that of the two horses. It would be next to impossible to track the horses out of camp, far as she could see. The whole area around the camp was a maze of tracks. Moreover, there were scores of tracks on the route they were following; it led toward the little canyon two miles down the valley where Tackleman had set up a second guard. It consisted of three men to a watch and it had been changed several times.

They saw the light from the lanterns that marked the place when they were still half a mile away. Jackson turned the horses toward the center of the valley and they passed at a distance but close enough so that Laura Jean glimpsed the shadowy figure of a guard as he moved in front of a lantern.

Looking straight ahead and trying to seem casual about it, Laura Jean began to whistle "Onward Christian Soldiers," remembering that it was what she was whistling when the posse first overtook her. She began weakly and then tried to get a little bravura into it.

Jackson laughed. "I'm hardly going to shoot you for that, but I'd just as soon you stopped it."

She did, feeling a little foolish. Even if the guards could hear her, they would probably think she was some cowhand on his way home from the shindig.

"What do you want with a hostage?" she asked.

"Seems like a good idea."

"Why me?"

"You were readily available, Miss Dundee. Besides, I enjoy your company. How does it happen that you didn't go on to Langtown?"

"I got a job in Table City."

"I see. What kind of job?"

She told him about it. She had been terrified when he grabbed her, but she found herself talking to him just as if they were friends or something. The more she talked, the less afraid she felt. She even found herself chatting about riding in the Mercedes and spending the night at Tackleman's lodge on the lake.

"Ah, the very rich," Jackson said. "Would you like to be rich, Miss Dundee?"

"Wouldn't everybody?"

"The things of this world—we all want them, don't we?"

"Sure. I want a whole lot of them."

"All you can get?"

"Yes, I guess so." She said thoughtfully, "There's something else I want more, I guess. I want to learn everything I can about everything. I want to go on learning all my life. My mother used to say that's the secret of happiness."

"A wise woman."

"The trouble was Mother never had time to do

anything but work. For my brother and me. She loved to read, but she was always so tired she fell asleep."

"Bless her."

"Sometimes you talk like a preacher," Laura Jean said. He made no reply, and she asked, "Would you have shot me back there in camp if I'd screamed?"

"Of course."

"I don't believe you would have."

"That's a dangerous assumption, Miss Dundee."

"You said that little gun you held against my stomach was cocked. After you got me out of camp, you took it away and I could see it wasn't."

"I eased down the hammer. You just didn't notice."

They crossed a creek and could see a shadowy gap in the ridge to the east. That was where the homestead was, she thought, where she had bought back Flag. She thought that they might turn into the gap, but they didn't.

"Are you a professional gambler?" she asked.

"You might say that." He was in a strangely cheerful mood and there was a laugh in his voice. "Why?"

"Sheriff Briley was trying to figure out who you were and where you were headed. He thought you might be a gambler. Or an accountant. Or an engineer."

"Sheriff Briley," he said. "A dangerous man."

"Dangerous? He didn't even go out looking for you today."

"He stayed in camp?"

"I think he went to Table City and got a shave."

He brought the horses to a stop, then rode around the front of her horse and handed her off rein to her. He made no explanation, but the move seemed sensible because a horse usually follows more easily when led by only one rein.

"Briley," he said as they moved on. He stared straight ahead and seemed almost to be talking to himself. "I am more afraid of Briley than all the rest of them put together."

That seemed to her a strange thing to say. You'd better be afraid of Lloyd Tackleman, she thought.

He seemed to be in no special hurry, and they rode mostly at a walk. Every once in a while he slipped a watch from his pocket and consulted it. He had a hard time reading it, tipping it every which way to catch the starlight. He also kept looking around, studying the ridge on one side of the narrow valley and the black hulk of the War Bonnets on the other. They had traveled for more than an hour, she guessed. They must be half way to the stage road. He slowed, looking down at his horse as if something was wrong with it. After a little way, he reined up.

"My cinch is loose," he said.

He dismounted, casually twisting her left rein around his saddlehorn. He turned up the stirrup and hooked it on the horn over the rein. He stepped back, bending a little as he untied the latigo.

She gently touched heels to flanks, urging her horse forward a step. He bent behind his saddle, fussing with the cinch ring. She reached for the rein and got it, pulled it cautiously. It slid around the saddlehorn under the stirrup and came free. She wheeled her horse to the right and kicked it into a gallop.

Bending low, she waited for a shot, thinking she was a fool and that she was going to die. Gaining hope with every leap of the horse, she looked back. He had mounted and was coming after her but was farther back then she had expected. She whipped her horse with rein ends and prayed that it was faster and stronger than the other. Then he was no longer coming after her, and she saw that he had dismounted again. Evidently, there was still something wrong with his cinch.

XX

The Journal of Patrick H. Briley, Sheriff of Hooper County, Montana.

Cobweb Canyon, Bannock County, Mont., Monday, June 10, 1901, Evening.

I am told by D. Wales, labor agitator, that Yates is a card sharp. Regardless of whether that is true, I have a feeling the man is dissembling in some way, and I record the following facts and observations:

Yates's account of the robbery is unsatisfactory in some way I cannot pinpoint. He is consistent and all that, but my instinct tells me he is falsifying some of the facts or leaving them out, or both.

Yates and A. Corner, banker, are old friends and business associates. Yates tried to conceal that fact. Corner admitted it readily enough, but my instinct tells me that he also was far from candid.

Yates brought whiskey into this camp in spite of my admonition not to. At present he appears to be drunk, but on closer observation he may be pretending to be drunk.

D. Wales has written a document which sets forth alleged facts in regard to financial hocus pocus in certain mining circles. Wales's informant is R. Hogan, chief accountant for Cyclops-Umatilla. Hogan was recruited by persons from North American Land & Livestock, led by L. Tackleman, and aided them in a takeover of Cyclops. He was recruited in Denver and was involved in various irregular accounting operations there, in New York, and in Butte, where he is at present.

He states (according to Wales) that Tackleman's crowd infiltrated management, largely by bribery. They then held back production, falsified figures, and depressed the value of Cyclops common stock so that North American could buy it up cheaply. By the time of the annual meeting this spring, North American owned approximately 35% of the outstanding stock. By means of these holdings plus proxies obtained from other stockholders, North American was able to complete the takeover.

Previously, the Cyclops president and chairman of the board. A. J. Laslow, had been forced out by Tackleman's infiltrators, who accused him of embezzlement. According to Hogan, this was a frame-up. It was necessary to disgrace Laslow, Hogan says, to prevent him from obtaining enough proxies on his own to beat the North American bunch.

Cyclops's headquarters is in New York. It has branch offices in Denver and Butte. It was discovered that Laslow had personal bank accounts in the last two cities that he used only when he was present in those cities. The frame-up was accomplished by embezzling a large amount of cash and depositing that exact amount in Laslow's Denver account.

Wales states that Hogan has evidence of the frame-up in the form of a receipted deposit slip and a canceled check with Laslow's forged endorsement. These documents were supposed to have been destroyed but were not.

Hogan also told Wales that Tackleman's people at Cyclops are preparing an elaborate scheme to transfer Cyclops's most valuable mining properties to a corporation called Tenstone. This corporation was formed and is 90% owned by Tackleman, a fact not known to North American directors who are not in Tackleman's camp. The transfer will leave Cyclops bankrupt. Its stockholders, including North American will lose millions. Tackleman will walk off with the spoils.

It is clear that Hogan is a bitter, disgruntled person (with good reason, according to Wales). But it seems to me that he has delusions of grandeur, as they say. He's not interested in stopping the financial manipulations but only in gathering evidence along the way that he thinks will enable him to someday bring Tackleman down.

It is worth mentioning that Wales considers Laslow "a decent man." In childhood he knew what it was to be poor, Wales says, and is more sympathetic to the needs of the working class than most corporation heads. Coming from Wales, that is high praise.

It is interesting to note that this is the same Laslow who, years ago, was involved with Yates and Corner in the sale of a maverick railroad spur to the NP. He was then a young mining engineer with Umatilla

Slate and Ore. When Cyclops and Umatilla merged, he evidently went quickly to the top.

Thanks to whiskey and a wagonload of Jezebels, this camp has turned into a stompfest sorely in need of pacification, a chore I declined to undertake even though Hornbill is tree-climbing drunk.

XXI

After the first hard spurt, Laura Jean's horse wasn't able to keep up much of a pace. It seemed to her that it took forever to reach camp. When she did, the fires had died down and the musicians and the girls were not in evidence. Except for a lone drunk staggering around with a lantern, the party was over. The drunk turned out to be Hornbill, trying to change the watch and unable to find the relief guards. Laura Jean ignored him, rode up to the Mercedes, and slid off her horse.

Hurley was asleep in the front seat, Tackleman in back. She had to shake him hard to wake him. He sat up, throwing off the blanket he'd pulled over him.

"I dozed off. Wondered where you'd bedded down."

"I was abducted! He abducted me! I got away."

Nobody had even missed her, and now Tackleman stared at her as if she were babbling nonsense. She was on the verge of tears.

"Jackson!" she said. "He's miles down the valley!"

By the time she got it all out, he had wakened Hurley and sent him to rouse the camp and to find

Hornbill. He pulled switches and set levers and cranked the car. She sat behind the wheel and followed his directions and they got it started.

The camp stirred uncertainly. Hurley came back leading Hornbill by the elbow. Tackleman applied matches to the carbide headlamps. He was hatless, his hair disheveled. The glow of the lamps gave him an eerie, unworldly look.

Briley came up, unruffled as ever. Tackleman spoke with steely evenness. "We'll take the car. If Jackson stays in the valley, we'll run him down by sunrise. Get the posse saddled up and follow us. Bring our horses in case he goes into rough country again."

He pulled on his hunting cap, picked up his Sharps. He ushered Hornbill into the front seat. Hurley was to drive, and Laura Jean got out of the car so he could get behind the wheel.

"Get in," Tackleman said to her. "We'll ride in back."

She took a deep breath and didn't move. Jim Smoke strolled into the glow of the headlamps, looking sleepy.

"Get in," Tackleman said to him. "Squeeze into the front beside the sheriff. Get aboard, Laura Jean."

She gave a shake of her head so slight that she herself was hardly aware of it. He climbed into the back seat and slid over to the far side. He held his rifle in his right hand, rested on the seat with muzzle pointed to the sky. His left arm lay along the back of the seat. He smiled his handsome smile.

The camp had come to life with the snorts of horses and oaths of men catching mounts and saddling up.

A man got kicked in the groin and screamed and rolled on the ground. Men stood around him and watched his agony, unable to do anything for him. When he rolled to his knees and vomited, they turned away.

"Laura Jean," Tackleman said, still smiling. "Come on. Get in."

"I'm not going," she said.

"Good Lord, girl, this is it. The end of the chase. The kill."

"The kill," she said. "No, thank you."

Tackleman's smile was gone. "Get in here."

"No, Mr. Tackleman."

"Laura Jean—"

"No."

His look was one she would never forget. He wouldn't allow himself angry words, she thought. He was too controlled for that. And the look was enough, as cold, as piercing, and as final as a blade.

For a moment she was certain that he would reach for her and pull her into the car. But someone was beside her. Timbo. To her surprise then, Tackleman did allow himself words, and they were flat and ugly.

"Well, you grubby little tease."

He made a throwing gesture at Hurley, and the Mercedes moved off. Laura Jean turned to Timbo, and something passed between them. He laid an arm across his sister's shoulders. They watched the lights of the car seek out a course and then gather speed down the valley.

"No," Laura Jean Dundee sighed into the darkness.

XXII

Jackson galloped after Laura Jean for a short distance, riding hard as if he were desperately trying to catch her. Then he pulled up and for the second time dismounted and pretended there was something wrong with his cinch.

He watched the darkness swallow her racing figure and listened until the beat of her horse could no longer be heard. He consulted his watch and made calculations regarding distance and the time till dawn. Leisurely, he mounted his horse and rode down the center of the flat, narrow, sage-dappled valley.

The earth was baked, barren except for sage and occasional tufts of grass. He glanced back at his trail, which was shallow but distinct, easy enough to follow even at night. He stayed in the open and made no effort to confuse or conceal it.

He continued straight down the valley, drifting a bit toward the ridge to his left. Light was seeping into the sky above the ridge when he reached a chain of rock outcrops that rose from the valley floor in a saber-shaped pattern a hundred yards long. It was just as he remembered it—not a solid formation but a series of ragged projections with gaps of several yards between them. They varied in height from a few inches to a dozen feet.

He rode into the concave side of the pattern, pointing toward a fifteen-foot gap a little to the right of its center. Instead of riding through, however, he stopped and dismounted just before he reached the gap. Here, he uncinched his saddle, slid it from the horse, and dropped it. Vaulting aboard the animal, he rode on through the gap, leaving the saddle behind.

He rode ahead for a quarter of a mile, leaving a straight and clearly visible trail. Then he made a wide circle to the west that brought him back toward the chain of outcrops from that direction. Just before he reached them he rode into a little gully screened by brush, tied his horse here, and made his way on foot back to the rocks.

Approaching on the convex side of the chain, he chose a place about fifty feet from the gap he had passed through. He stood behind a rock about five feet high with a ragged top surface. He found two melon-size chunks of rock and placed them on top, a few inches apart. He checked his rifle and laid it beside them.

He waited on his feet, pacing behind the outcrop, not wanting to risk falling asleep. It was chilly in this first smoky light of day. He rubbed his hands together, put them in his pockets to warm them. He did a little jig to get his circulation going, and smiled as he thought of Wales prancing and leaping.

Wales will know, he thought. No, he already knows, he's guessed. That makes three. Too many, but they all are involved, too. Accessories before and after the fact. More important, they are all men of the same rare stamp. Men who make their own rules, but who truly have rules and do not break them.

Thoughts, memories spun through his head like numbers on a roulette wheel, the ivory ball leaping from one to another. It settled on Grandfather.

Why? Grandfather would have asked.

He's an evil man.

Who says so? You?

He's an enemy.

That's better. For me that would be good enough. But choose an honorable way.

I did.

You're sure?

Yes . . . No. He never had a chance.

Stop it, Jackson told himself. The thinking has been done, the decision made, the sentence pronounced. . . .

He spotted the Mercedes as it topped a little lift of ground a mile and a half away, its lights a probing barb in the early dimness. He picked up dirt and spat on it, working it into a dark paste that he smeared on his forehead, his nose, his cheeks above his beard. War paint, he thought. But it was just as well that those who hadn't already seen his face didn't get too good a look at it. He checked his rifle, warmed his hands again.

The car came on swiftly, following the clear trace he had left, swerving to avoid sagebrush. He bent close to the outcrop, peering from between the chunks of rock he had placed there, eager to make out the passengers.

He looked for the Dundee girl, saw that she wasn't among them, and muttered his relief. Tackleman was alone in the back seat. His driver was at the wheel, and there were two others in the seat with him. The tracker and, of course, the swaggering little sheriff of Bannock county.

The car slowed as it drew into the arc made by the outcrops. It approached the saddle he had left behind and stopped. The tracker got out to examine the saddle. Tackleman stood up, holding his rifle, watching the tracker.

The tracker stopped, suddenly suspicious. He turned motioning with his arms and calling to the others to get down.

He was too late. Jackson's bead was between the eye and the ear, an inch above the edge of the hunting cap. He squeezed the trigger. Tackleman's head jerked to the right with the impact of the bullet. He fell forward on top of Hornbill and rolled out of the far side of the car.

"Freeze!" Jackson yelled. He snick-snacked a fresh cartridge into the chamber. "Move a finger and you're dead."

At the crack of the shot, the tracker had dropped to the ground. He was on his stomach, facing the car. The driver was motionless, hands on the wheel. Hornbill stood up, bringing a rifle up clumsily, looking around in a wild, confused way.

"Drop it! You've got one second!"

Hornbill didn't hear, and the driver said, "He's got us covered. Drop the gun." With a pushing motion, the sheriff threw the rifle from the car. Still looking around, trying to locate Jackson, he raised his hands.

"Get out," Jackson ordered. "On this side. Leave the motor running. . . . Now lie down. Face down, hands out in front of you."

He climbed over the outcrop. He relieved Hornbill of his revolver, tossing it and the rifle into the car. He searched Hurley, removing a stubby revolver from a pocket. Jim Smoke was not armed. Jackson threw a few quick words at him, and then went around the car for his look at Tackleman. Fighting off a surge of nausea, he climbed behind the wheel of the Mercedes, ground gears, and drove past the saddle through the gap between the outcrops and on down the valley.

When the horsemen galloped up, Hurley was sitting beside Tackleman's body, having covered it with his linen duster. Hornbill sat a little way off, looking stunned and sick. He got to his feet as Briley dismounted, but he just shook his head and said nothing. The scene spoke for itself.

Briley drew back the duster and had his brief look. Jim Smoke came through the chain of outcrops from the other side, leading a horse. He picked up Jackson's saddle and swung it onto the horse's back. Briley walked over to him.

"Jackson's horse?"

Jim nodded. "The one he stole . . . Funny thing— before he drove off, he told me where he'd tied the horse. And he told me he left another horse tied in Cobweb canyon last night. Said it was in a side canyon a little way above the guard post. Funny."

Briley agreed. It did seem peculiar for a murderer running for his life to be concerned about the well being of a couple of horses.

It was decided that Hornbill would head straight for Table City and get on the telephone and the telegraph. Briley told Em Foster to go with him and do the telephone talking.

Except for Jim Smoke, Briley and the rest of the posse rode south after the car. "You don't need me to track a goddamn motor car," Jim said.

The tire tracks turned right at the stage road and led Briley's party back through the War Bonnets and across the St. Terry. Farther along, there was a fork in the road with one branch dropping off toward Sperrysville. The Mercedes had taken the other, which led eventually to Butte.

Briley sent the posse to Sperrysville with instructions to get on the telephone with the word that Jackson was on the Butte road. He announced that he would go on after the Mercedes alone.

"This outfit is in no shape to travel fast," he insisted. "You'd just hold me up. Alone, I can probably find a change of horses now and then and make pretty fair time."

XXIII

The Journal of Patrick H. Briley, Sheriff of Hooper County, Montana.

Golden Trumpet Mine, Silver Bow County, Mont., Tuesday, June 11, 1901, Evening.

Followed tire tracks to this deserted diggings one mile off the stage road and an estimated seven miles from Butte. I found the motor car here, half-hidden in an old shed. Also found a small pasture and a brass watering trough that has been cleaned out and filled within the last week or ten days. Also found fresh horse manure and a set of tracks pointing back to the stage road. They were half a day old and undoubtedly obliterated on the road by later traffic.

In the old mine office I found a wash basin, soap, and towel, recently used. There is soap residue in the basin and evidence that Jackson has shaved. He may also have changed clothes and chucked his old ones down a shaft.

I managed to obtain a change of horse three times along the road today, but it was not enough. I will spend the night at this place, both man and animal being on the verge of exflunctification.

Butte, Silver Bow County, Mont., Wednesday, June 12, 1901, Evening.

Newspaper headlines are three inches high. I arrived here this morning and have been annoyed by representatives of the press ever since.

Sheriff Hap Bensen informs me he was contacted by telephone early yesterday afternoon. It took that long for Hornbill to get back to Table City and put a call through. By that time, Bensen figures, Jackson could already have been in this city. Or beyond.

Bensen reports that yesterday's eastbound limited was late and was further delayed by the need to pick up a private car, and was still in the yards when he got the phone call. He and deputies conducted a thorough search of the train. They found two passengers that fit Jackson's description but who turned out to have been on the train since it left Seattle, confirmed by the conductor. It is my understanding that the same train was again searched at Billings by the sheriff and deputies of Yellowstone County.

Bensen has put on extra deputies here and they, along with city police and yard dicks, are searching every inch of every train that leaves Butte, passenger and freight.

Bensen has also canvased all liveries, stage offices, hotels, boarding houses, and brothels. All leads have come to nothing. An early one, a report of a man who left a horse and buggy at a livery barn early yesterday afternoon, turned out to lead to S. Gilly, Tackleman's aide. Gilly was found at the North American office here, and he collapsed when given the news that Tackleman was dead.

The only thing of any substance whatsoever that has turned up is a horse found in a gulch on the edge of town, nobody claiming ownership of said animal. I determined that its tracks match those I found at the Golden Trumpet yesterday. So it now seems certain that Jackson is, or was, in Butte. He may be in hiding or he may have passed through. Customs officers on the Canadian border and the Royal Canadian Mounted Police have been alerted.

This evening Mrs. Tackleman and Mrs. Gilly arrived by private stagecoach with Tackleman's embalmed remains, which will be accompanied by Mrs. Tackleman to the East for burial.

Butte, Silver Bow County, Mont., Saturday, June 15, 1901, Evening.

Representatives of the press from eastern states have arrived in this city, also three Pinkerton men, hired perhaps by North American Land & Livestock. The Pinkertons questioned me at length. I found them patronizing and impatient. I answered all questions to the best of my ability but volunteered no theories, which they didn't want anyway.

Reading back over this journal, I was struck by an omission and called on Sheriff Bensen to supply the information, which he did readily. The private car that was picked up by the NP eastbound here last

Tuesday was that of A. J. Laslow, former president and board chairman of Cyclops-Umatilla. I checked with the railroad and learned that Laslow arrived here on June 4. He went trout fishing down on the Madison, the NP traffic manager said, and the car was held in the yards until his return.

Sheriff Bensen states that the private car was searched last Tuesday along with the rest of the train, Laslow being friendly and cooperative with deputies. One of the deputies gave Laslow the news that Tackleman was dead and that they were searching for his killer. According to the deputy, Laslow was surprised and asked several questions which the deputy was unable to answer at that time.

I see nothing to be gained by remaining longer in this city and will return to Hooper County by stage tomorrow.

Hooper City, Hooper County, Mont., Tuesday, June 18, 1901, Evening.

Interviewed H. Swanson, hotel clerk. He is still not oath-taking certain as to what happened the night of June 8-9, but clings to the impression he was not cold-cocked by Jackson and that there was a fourth person in Yates's hotel room.

The local paper has a telegraph story about a bank robbery in Butte yesterday perpetrated by a man that the tellers claim answers Jackson's description. A telegram from Sheriff Bensen informs me, however, that the robber has been apprehended, along with the loot, and that he is five-foot-two and cross-eyed.

Today I purchased 300 shares of Cyclops-Umatilla common stock, which has dropped to 2Î.

Hooper City, Hooper County, Mont., Friday, June 21, 1901, Evening.

Sheriff Harry Hornbill of Bannock County was in town today claiming to be in pursuit of a drifter who passed a gold-plated nickel as a five-dollar goldpiece in a Sperrysville saloon. He was sober but greatly distressed, being pestered by Pinkertons and representatives of the press, who do not treat him sympathetically in their newspapers. He is worried about his popularity with the voters and says he needs to make some news that will restore his local prestige. I told him to get after that town marshal with the pet rattlesnake.

He mentioned that a wounded horse abandoned by Jackson in the War Bonnets has been found. When I questioned him in detail, he said that Amos Corner hired a cowhand to go get it and that said horse is now at Corner's C Dot ranch, has been treated by a veterinarian, and is in good shape. The curious thing to me is how Corner knew the location of the horse. If I was a Pinkerton, I would look into this, but I dare say Corner will have a plausible explanation.

Hooper City, Hooper County, Mont., Thursday, July 4, 1901, Midnight.

It is evident from the newspapers that the Tackleman crowd's control of Cyclops-Umatilla collapsed with his death. Gilly and two other members of the board of directors resigned, apparently unable to carry the load without Tackleman's power over men and money.

Executives sympathetic to the deposed Laslow (or maybe just running for cover) have now unearthed evidence that cleared him of false allegations and put the blame where it belongs. He was reinstated by the directors and a special stockholders meeting will take place later this month.

Cyclops mines reopened Monday. The common stock went up to 8 when the announcement was made last week but dropped to 6 when it was learned that workers will receive a dollar-a-day raise in wages, effective immediately.

Three fireworks injuries today, none fatal. Two children, one cowhand. Em Foster lost a haystack tonight, due to a skyrocket.

Hooper City, Hooper County, Mont., Sunday, July 28, 1901, Evening.

Jim Smoke was in town this last week, having been hired by North American to track down a rogue grizzly that has been killing sheep on their N3 holdings south of here. He states that Laura Jean Dundee is living with her brother near Langtown and is working at the Blue Ribbon Home Cooking Restaurant. He also states that she is the recipient of a new scholarship to be awarded every fourth year to a promising female and that will pay room, board, and tuition at Montana State College as long as she keeps up her grades.

Following a hunch, I exchanged several telegrams

with the sheriff of Missoula County, who contacted college officials. The scholarship was endowed by Cyclops-Umatilla. After putting severe pressure on said officials, he was able to learn that a secret condition of the endowment was that Laura Jean Dundee be the first recipient.

Pinkerton detectives are no longer on the case. I don't know exactly how long ago they were called off, but it seems they had been employed by Cyclops-Umatilla and not North American Land & Livestock as I supposed.

Cyclops-Umatilla common stock has reached 16½.

Hooper City, Hooper County, Mont., Thursday, August 8, 1901, Evening.

For several weeks I have been trying to look into the background of A. J. Laslow, writing letters to everybody I could think of who might know something about him. Until now, I have had no success, not even getting a reply from D. Wales, who hinted he knew something about the man's childhood and who owes me a favor. Today, however, I heard from a newspaperman in Idaho Falls, an old friend, who gave me some solid information.

Laslow is the illegitimate son of an Army officer and a quarterbreed Indian woman. She died while he was still an infant, and he was raised on the Fort Hall reservation by his grandparents. When he was fifteen, his father, recently widowed and without other offspring, acknowledged the boy and provided for his education. Laslow graduated from the Colorado School of Mines, went to work as a mining engineer for Umatilla Slate & Ore, and eventually rose to control of Cyclops-Umatilla as stated elsewhere.

Now you take a man who is by and large a decent man, who has a soft spot for horses and bright, ambitious, little girls. It seems to me that if such a man felt an overwhelming necessity to deprive another man of his life, he would have to kill him himself. If he hired somebody else to do it, he couldn't live with himself in this world or the next.

Now suppose this man didn't want the killing to look like a planned assassination, even though that was what it was. It seems to me that he might figure out a way to make it look like an ironic accident—the hunter being killed by the hunted.

He would need help, of course. I think he got together with two old gambling cronies and former business partners he could trust. He needed Corner to map the country for him, to buy up Cyclops stock, and perhaps to provide a refuge in the Table City area in case something went wrong. He needed Yates to stage the robbery and initiate the manhunt.

Yates was on his way out of his hotel room, meaning to go down the hall to the fire stairs, when he bumped into Swanson. Swanson is right about Jackson not being the one who slugged him, but he is wrong about there being a fourth man in the room. Yates slugged him. He then went to the fire stairs and down to the street, rolling to get himself covered with dust as if he had been thrown out of the window that Jackson smashed out with a chair.

With roundup over, the town in a Saturday night mood, and Yates offering a $698 reward, it was inevitable that a chase party would form. Jackson led it into Bannock County, right under Tackleman's nose, sure that he couldn't resist joining it.

It seems to me that he knew about the car from the beginning, too, and counted on it for a getaway. I believe he planned to lead the posse into the War Bonnets and then go over the pass. The only chance of cutting him off then would have been with the car, and his original plan was to kill Tackleman on the other side of the pass. Tackleman outmaneuvered him there, however, and blocked the pass. The man who called himself Jackson had to find another way to get Tackleman out ahead of the party in the car.

It worked. There has been no suspicion of involvement by business rivals of Tackleman. Press and public believe he was done in by a maverick named Jackson, who appeared in Hooper City about June 5, and disappeared in the vicinity of Butte, June 11.

My case is circumstantial, but it doesn't have to be. All I have to do is go to New York for a look at Andrew Jackson Laslow face to face. I might make myself a reputation and be a famous character in my old age, but I have lived too close to the plain life to covet that now. It is my position that the only illegal act the man committed in my county was a busted window, a misdemeanor.

I will not stand for reelection. I own a half section in a warm little valley on the Singing Dog, sheltered land where the hay grows wild and deer come to winter. I will build a house with a porch to face the sunset, a place to sit on summer evenings and write things down. I have known the Frontier as a place of foolishness and wisdom and a freedom so big it sometimes scares you. It is coming to an end now, and I will try to put on paper for my grandchildren what my little piece of it was like, exact and in detail, but I would like to capture the inexactness of it, too, the feel of it, and the fulfillment it brought to a sometimes faithful servant of the Law.

It is my simple belief that the Good Lord will make things happen for the best, if the public will let him.

BOLD HEROES OF THE UNTAMED NORTHWEST!
THE SCARLET RIDERS
by Ian Anderson

#1: CORPORAL CAVANNAGH   (1161, $2.50)
Joining the Mounties was Cavannagh's last chance at a new life. Now he would stop either an Indian war, or a bullet—and out of his daring and courage a legend would be born!

#2: THE RETURN OF CAVANNAGH   (1817, $2.25)
A private army of bloodthirsty outlaws are hired to massacre the Mounties at Fort Walsh. Joined by the bold Indian fighter Cavannagh, the Riders prepare for the deadliest battle of their lives!

#3: BEYOND THE STONE HEAPS   (1884, $2.50)
Fresh from the slaughter at the Little Big Horn, the Sioux cross the border into Canada. Only Cavannagh can prevent the raging Indian war that threatens to destroy the Scarlet Riders!

#4: SERGEANT O'REILLY   (1977, $2.50)
When an Indian village is reduced to ashes, Sergeant O'Reilly of the Mounties risks his life and career to help an avenging Stoney chief and bring a silver-hungry murderer to justice!

#5: FORT TERROR   (2125, $2.50)
Captured by the robed and bearded killer monks of Fort Terror, Parsons knew it was up to him, and him alone, to stop a terrifying reign of anarchy and chaos by the deadliest assassins in the territory—and continue the growing legend of The Scarlet Riders!

POWELL'S ARMY
BY TERENCE DUNCAN

#1: UNCHAINED LIGHTNING   (1994, $2.50)
Thundering out of the past, a trio of deadly enforcers dispenses its own brand of frontier justice throughout the untamed American West! Two men and one woman, they are the U.S. Army's most lethal secret weapon—they are POWELL'S ARMY!

#2: APACHE RAIDERS   (2073, $2.50)
The disappearance of seventeen Apache maidens brings tribal unrest to the violent breaking point. To prevent an explosion of bloodshed, Powell's Army races through a nightmare world south of the border—and into the deadly clutches of a vicious band of Mexican flesh merchants!

#3: MUSTANG WARRIORS   (2171, $2.50)
Someone is selling cavalry guns and horses to the Comanche—and that spells trouble for the bluecoats' campaign against Chief Quanah Parker's bloodthirsty Kwahadi warriors. But Powell's Army are no strangers to trouble. When the showdown comes, they'll be ready—and someone is going to die!

#4: ROBBERS ROOST   (2285, $2.50)
After hijacking an army payroll wagon and killing the troopers riding guard, Three-Fingered Jack and his gang high-tail it into Virginia City to spend their ill-gotten gains. But Powell's Army plans to apprehend the murderous hardcases before the local vigilantes do—to make sure that Jack and his slimy band stretch hemp the legal way!

ACTION ADVENTURE